'Don't be a bad

'I'm not——' Emma's
by Dominick's mouth
of asserting herself
with short, hungry snatches of passion which
aroused her more headily than she could ever
have imagined.

'You want me too,' Dominick said on a thick
groan. 'Admit it, Emma.'

'Yes,' she whispered faintly. 'I want you...'

Dear Reader

The new year is a time for resolutions and here at Mills & Boon we will continue to give you the best romances we possibly can. We're sure the year's books will live up to your expectations! This month we hope to shake off the winter chills by taking you to some wonderful exotic locations—Morocco, the Bahamas and the Caribbean. Closer to home, this is the time of year when we celebrate love and lovers, with St Valentine's Day. Which of our heroes would you like to spend the day with? Until next month,

The Editor

Having abandoned her first intended career for marriage, **Rosalie Ash** spent several years as a bilingual personal assistant to the managing director of a leisure group. She now lives in Warwickshire with her husband, and daughters Kate and Abby, and her lifelong enjoyment of writing has led to her career as a novelist. Her interests include languages, travel and research for her books, reading, and visits to the Royal Shakespeare Theatre in nearby Stratford-upon-Avon. Other pleasures include swimming, yoga and country walks.

Recent titles by the same author:

AN IMPORTED WIFE
APOLLO'S LEGEND
MYTHS OF THE MOON

VENGEFUL BRIDE

BY

ROSALIE ASH

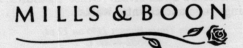

MILLS & BOON LIMITED
ETON HOUSE, 18-24 PARADISE ROAD
RICHMOND, SURREY TW9 1SR

*MILLS & BOON and the Rose Device
are trademarks of the publisher.*

*First published in Great Britain 1994
by Mills & Boon Limited*

© Rosalie Ash 1994

*Australian copyright 1994   Philippine copyright 1995
This edition 1995*

ISBN 0 263 78872 5

*Set in Times Roman 11½ on 12 pt.
01-9502-44960 C*

Made and printed in Great Britain

CHAPTER ONE

HER prospective employer was tall, broad-shouldered, and darkly attractive. Emma watched him rise to his feet, circle the vast mahogany desk and cross the carpeted study towards her, and for a few moments her nerve failed...

'Miss Stuart. Come and sit down.' He spoke pleasantly, his voice husky, full of that deeply ingrained male confidence which came from generations of wealth and power. Catching her breath sharply, she felt the warm strength of his hand as he clasped hers in greeting.

'Thank you.' Weakly, silently ordering her wobbling legs to carry her, she went to sit on the round-backed chair he was indicating. She crossed her legs. The skirt of her smart violet wool suit felt too short. Furiously she uncrossed her knees again and clamped them firmly together, tucking her ankles under the chair. She had the annoying impression that he was watching her discomfiture with veiled amusement.

'Would you like tea? Coffee?'

'Tea would be lovely.' She smiled coolly. She had her feelings under control now. Discovering that Dominick Fleetwood in the flesh was a glorious cross between Mel Gibson and Kevin

Costner had thrown her initially, but she had enough inward motivation to handle that...

He was relaying the order for tea to the elderly housekeeper who'd shown her in. When the housekeeper had gone, he sat on the edge of the desk, and eyed Emma expressionlessly.

'So you're a fully qualified archivist?' His eyes were a stunning shade of blue, she registered, meeting their probing gaze with her own clear, deceptively mild grey ones.

'I am.'

'You don't look like one.'

She smothered a desire to laugh.

'What does an archivist look like?' she enquired gravely.

'I pictured someone dusty, flat-chested and a confirmed spinster,' he informed her, equally deadpan. 'Whereas I suspect that behind the disguise of those steel-rimmed glasses and raked-back hairstyle *you* are definitely nubile.'

The audacious chauvinism almost took her breath away. Did he seriously expect her to want the job, when he said things like that? But anticipation of the tailor-made perfection of the job, and a secret she'd no intention of revealing just yet, kept her glued to the chair like a prisoner.

'Whether that's supposed to be compliment or insult,' she managed calmly, 'I'll do you a favour and ignore it.'

The gentian-blue gaze narrowed speculatively. His eyes were long and dark-lashed, and unnervingly intense. In spite of her composure, she felt herself begin to prickle with awareness as he slid his gaze over the pale, set oval of her face, the neat shine of chestnut hair wound into a prim bun, the conservative cut of her suit not quite concealing voluptuous breasts and hips, a swoopingly narrow waist and long slim legs which went on forever...

In turn, she gazed back at him, taking involuntary note of the fine grey cloth of his city suit, the immaculate whiteness of his shirt. His skin tone was almost Mediterranean-dark. His hair was thick and black and wavy, cut short on top and curling slightly into his nape. He'd look good wearing a gold earring, she told herself tartly. There was a dangerous gypsy air about him, at odds with his upper-class lineage...

She had the sudden, sinking feeling that he knew exactly who she was, knew exactly why she felt this burning curiosity to see Fleetwood Manor... After all, he was a brilliant barrister, fêted in London as one of the youngest and brightest to be called to the bar. Weren't barristers supposed to be gifted at reading people's thoughts and motives? At knowing everything about everyone?

But that was crazy. Dominick Fleetwood couldn't possibly remember her. She certainly didn't remember him. She'd been born here on the Fleetwood estate, but they'd have left when she was about five. And Dominick would have been away at school...

And besides, how could Dominick Fleetwood know why she was here, when she didn't even quite know herself?

The evidence she had, from things her father had said, was strong but not conclusive...

She'd braced herself for some withering comment after her pert retort. But after what felt like an endless pause all he said, in a thoughtful voice, was, 'You realise the family records are stored in filthy old boxes, in all manner of spidery corners of the estate?'

'I'm sure they are.'

'Can you lift down heavy trunks of papers?'

'Yes. I'm quite strong.'

'Fleetwood Manor is in a lamentable state of repair. Bits of it may not have changed a great deal since the place was built in the fifteenth century. Will you mind working alone in the attics?'

'If you mean will I be frightened of ghosts or something, not in the least. History and the study of old houses, old records, is the great love of my life,' she heard herself enthusing, more frankly than she'd intended.

'So you're planning on being wedded to your work, Miss Stuart?' There was a wry note in his voice she couldn't identify.

'There are worse fates. At least that way a woman stays in control of her own existence,' she said quietly. Why was she letting him subtly open her up like this? This interview wasn't going at all the way she'd planned... She recalled his reputation as one of the country's foremost defence lawyers, information gleaned from newspapers and magazine articles. He'd been variously described as combining the rapier skills of a Jesuit catechist with the cunning of a wolf. Had she *ever* imagined she could somehow get the better of him, and thus get the better of the whole arrogant, destructive Fleetwood family...?

She bit her lip, irritated with her own vulnerability.

'You sound as if you've had bitter experience regarding the holy state of matrimony?' It was a cool probe. This time she didn't rise to the bait. She thought of her parents, but she shrugged and smiled blandly.

'I've never been married, if that's what you're asking.'

She'd arrived here prepared to feel coolly indifferent towards him, been briefly fazed by his devastating appearance, but in fact disliking him was going to be child's play. She already felt a stirring, fierce resentment towards him. Like father like son, she thought darkly. Womanising, patronising...

The door opened, and the housekeeper, a pleasant-faced grey-haired woman, brought in a tray of tea and biscuits. When they were alone again, he went back to sit behind the desk, leaning lazily back in the leather chair. His gaze was narrowed speculatively on her face.

'So, tell me more about why you want to come and work here,' he said calmly. 'You've just qualified in archive administration, and you're keen to earn more than the usual pittance paid to county archive assistants. Is that it, or is there another motive?'

The trace of cynical mockery seemed deliberately aimed to provoke. Emma kept her eyes on the tea-tray, a guilty sensation growing in the pit of her stomach. Her fears about his probing, dissecting skills were well justified, she realised nervously.

'As I've already said, I love history. I love historic houses. And I love deciphering old papers, uncovering the lives of past generations. What other motive do I need?'

'There should be enough skeletons in the Fleetwood closets to keep a scandal paper in business for months,' he commented, his drawl coolly unconcerned.

She felt her face heating slightly. Skeletons in closets? What a dry piece of upper-class understatement *that* was...

'Sounds as if I shall enjoy my job, Mr Fleetwood,' she commented mildly, hoping her casual tone would deter him from further interrogation, 'Or... should I be addressing you as Sir Dominick?' The cautious probe was deliberate. Newspaper reports could be wrong, after all...

Dominick Fleetwood's expression didn't alter.
'No. I'm just here on a kind of caretaker basis,' he said calmly. He seemed to consider for a few

moments, before continuing, 'Until my elder brother Richard can be traced.'

'Oh, yes...' It had all been there, in the newspaper stories. The search for the missing baronet, the older brother who'd automatically inherit the title and estate.

Maybe it was her slight hesitation, or just a faintly guilty air she was projecting, but he gave her a piercing look.

'Emma Stuart...' He repeated her name slowly. The frown creasing his forehead suddenly deepened. 'You're not, by any chance, related to the Stuarts who used to work here years ago? They had a child called Emma.'

Emma stared at him for a few seconds in mute dismay. She felt her stomach clench, then sink alarmingly. There was nothing else for it. She'd have to come clean.

'Yes. My parents worked here many years ago.'

Dominick's face remained unreadable. But he was staring at her with a suddenly sharpened curiosity.

'I remember them,' he said coolly. 'Jack Stuart was the gamekeeper, wasn't he? And a very good one. I remember my father admiring how he used to hatch up to two thousand grey partridge a week in the spring, ready for the autumn shoots.'

'Yes...' Colour was seeping into her face, and she felt a wave of annoyance. She had no reason to feel embarrassed about the past. She'd been only five when they'd left.

'I can hardly remember living here. But my father used to tell me stories about Fleetwood Manor, after we left...' She hesitated. Her father had made it sound so romantic, steeped in the past, full of ghosts and legends. As a child, she'd fantasised about this place...

'Stories?' Dominick persisted, his gaze quizzical.

'Catching poachers beneath a full moon, that sort of thing...' She smiled slightly at the melodramatic tinge to her statement. This was how her father had always talked about the manor. In sweeping, melodramatic adventure-story fashion. His passion for the place had been one reason for her own love of history. Now, though, since her father had died, it had a very different significance in her life...

Her brain was racing round in circles as she presented a calm façade. She'd been found out already, but, on the other hand, what had been found out? That she was Jack and Amy Stuart's daughter? Did that have any particular significance to Dominick Fleetwood?

Impossible to know what Dominick was thinking. How much he'd know. He clearly remembered her parents, but that didn't mean he knew everything that had gone on between his father and his various and numerous estate employees... She had to be very careful not to get paranoid...

'I'm intrigued,' he said at last. He picked up a pen from the blotter and slid it rhythmically through his fingers. His gaze was blandly thoughtful.

'What about?'

'Why didn't you mention living here as a child?'

It was a perfectly acceptable question, she told herself severely. And she didn't have a very good answer. 'Oh, what a tangled web we weave...' she lectured herself silently. Her throat dry as paper, she ran her tongue over her lips and swallowed abruptly. Shrugging slightly, she managed a laugh.

'It didn't occur to me. It was hardly relevant to the job specification!'

'But interesting, nevertheless.'

'I didn't imagine you'd be interested,' she countered flatly. She crossed her legs again, and reached with a commendably steady hand for her cup of tea. 'As I said, I can hardly remember living on the estate. My family wasn't here very long.'

'So is that why you've applied for this job? Out of curiosity? Nostalgia? A wish to revisit your childhood home?'

'Partly. Perhaps. But as you said just now, the money you're offering is a lot better than I could get elsewhere.'

'That's because I don't suffer fools gladly, Miss Stuart,' he informed her silkily. 'I'm busy in court for the majority of the week. And since I'm only caretaking this place until my brother is found and informed of his inheritance, I don't want

someone who works at a snail's pace. I'm prepared to pay a good salary for quick, efficient
work. For total commitment to the job. If I
thought you had some woolly, ulterior motive for
wanting to be here, I might be less enthusiastic.'
The gypsy-dark face was deadpan, but he was
definitely testing her in some way.

Hateful man, she fumed inwardly.

'If I'd come here claiming to have spent my
early childhood at Fleetwood Manor, you might
have thought I was angling for... for preferential
treatment or something. The past is... is quite
irrelevant. I'm quick, efficient, and my commitment will be total,' she assured him with as
cool a smile as she could muster. 'But can I
ask why you're so keen on speed? Are you in-
tending opening the manor to the public? Putting
interesting records on display?'

'Who knows?' His expression was lazily
amused. 'I personally would have no financial
need to open the house to visitors, Miss Stuart.
But let's just say that the situation regarding my
older brother is... unpredictable. He's been es-
tranged from my father for many years. Last
heard of, he'd dropped out of society in the wilds
of Tibet. There are certain eccentric conditions
laid down by Sir Robert which my brother will
have to be consulted on. Plus I have an impulsive
streak in my nature.' He grinned slightly, ar-
resting her suddenly with the revelation of even
white teeth and an attractive deepening of the
vertical furrows from nose to chin. 'I simply want

my family records sorted, deciphered, and safely stored for posterity.'

'Of course. I understand.'

'Good. If we both know where we stand, when can you start?'

'We . . . we haven't even talked about exact salary, or hours . . .'

He tilted a dark eyebrow at her determined expression.

'How much could you earn fresh from university as an assistant archivist with the council?'

She named a sum, and he gave a short laugh.

'I'll double it. Normal office hours, double pay for overtime. I'm not looking to employ some drab little Cinderella to drudge away in the attics, Miss Stuart.'

She blinked. Astonished, she heard herself saying weakly, 'No, well . . . would I be living in?'

'Naturally. One thing Fleetwood Manor isn't short of is accommodation. Unfortunately, most of it is uninhabitable. I'll show you where you'll be working and sleeping.'

He stood up, and strode decisively to the door. Emma followed. Panic returned. Should she be plunging into this? Should she be indulging her burning curiosity about her family's chequered past like this? Even if her father's story, the sad tale he'd related to her before he died, proved to be true, would she achieve anything with some vague notion of justice or revenge . . . ?

She followed the tall, athletic figure out of the study and into the picture-lined splendour of the manor's galleried hall. Up the sweeping blue-carpeted staircase, along a broad, creaking landing where the polished oak floorboards looked to be as old as the house, and past rows of cynical-looking Fleetwood males, each more swarthy and dangerous than the last, they finally made it to a smaller, more humble back stairway, and were up in the attics.

The view from up here was stunning, Emma registered bleakly, peering through dusty windows and noting sunlit acres of rolling Warwickshire countryside, just beginning to burgeon into the pale magnificence of spring.

Spring was a time for new beginnings, she told herself uneasily. Not a time for raking up the ashes of the past, torturing herself with a sentimental journey back to the start of her parents' tragic disintegration...

'A lot of the old family papers are up here,' Dominick was saying, pushing open a door to reveal a large room lined with shelves. There were some dusty old document cases, a big metal chest, an assortment of wooden storage boxes, some of them looking excitingly ancient. In spite of everything, Emma felt a *frisson* of anticipation at the historical riches yet to be uncovered. The manor had been in the Fleetwood family since the fifteenth century. She knew that from her father's stories. Who knew what fascinating information she might unearth...?

'You look like a cat surveying a dish of cream,' Dominick commented drily. 'You really like your chosen career, don't you?'

'I've always wanted to have the chance to do something like this,' she admitted, unable to hide her glow of enthusiasm.

'So this is your lucky year, Miss Stuart.' He led the way out of the attic room again, and they retraced their steps back down to the main landing. 'There's masses more in outhouses, and the old butler's pantry—it could take quite a while just getting it all together before you can sift through it.'

'Quite likely.'

'My housekeeper, Mrs Shields, has a strapping young grandson who can help to carry stuff around,' he added conversationally as he flung open a bedroom door and waved her inside.

'Thank you.' She found herself in a big square high-ceilinged bedroom, overlooking the front of the house. Large sash windows were draped in rich but faded gold velvet. A very high-looking four-poster bed with gold and cream covers occupied centre-stage. A door beyond stood open, with the end of an old-fashioned white claw-foot bath visible.

'Is this where I'll be sleeping?' It had such an air of grandeur, despite the thread-bare carpet and worn-looking fabrics, she could hardly believe it. Swinging round, she found Dominick Fleetwood's gaze gleaming with suppressed amusement.

'This, believe it or not, is the only usable guest-room at present. The rest have been sadly neglected. And there is one drawback,' he admitted calmly, leading the way to the bathroom. 'You share this bathroom with me.'

He flicked his hand idly towards another door, which presumably led into his bedroom beyond. Emma felt her stomach hollow with a combination of nerves, anger, and something else she couldn't identify...

'I'll be away most of the time. At my chambers in Lincoln's Inn. I may return some weekends. Will that cause any problems?' he persisted lazily. The blue gaze was unrelentingly amused.

'Not unless you expect me to scrub your back?' she quipped, on a dry laugh.

'Not part of the deal,' he agreed, with a grin, 'although I confess it's not an unattractive proposition.' He let his eyes slide deliberately down over her, lingering on her slender throat, the fullness of her breasts beneath the suit jacket.

'Speak for yourself,' she muttered, feeling a wave of heat creeping under her skin at his cool arrogance. He was standing about a foot away, but in the intimate confines of the bathroom he was suddenly much too close for her peace of mind. At well over six feet, he towered darkly over her own quite respectable height of five feet eight. With his hands pushed casually into his jacket pockets, his eyes calmly appraising her shaky composure, she was suddenly warmly aware of his masculinity. It conveyed itself so strongly, it seemed to hit her with the force of a tidal wave, a tidal wave of sensuality.

He was a brilliant 'jury' lawyer, people said. With her throat drying, she began to see how easily he could project the kind of powerful charisma needed to sway twelve jurors to vote for his client. Dominick was a daunting adversary. Maybe the missing Richard was the weaker of the two sons? Maybe, if the melodramatic notion of avenging her mother's honour and gaining her share of her inheritance had ever fleetingly occurred to her, her chance of extracting some sort of eye for an eye might have been more successfully directed at Richard, in any case?

'Are you all right, Miss Stuart?' He spoke softly, with just the merest hint of humour. She was ensnared in that narrowed blue gaze, and it was all she could do to catch her breath.

'Yes, I'm fine...'

'You look hot. Maybe you need some fresh air?'

'Yes. Maybe I do.' The look she gave him was politely veiled, but she had the sensation that he'd picked up on her vibrations of bitterness and resentment.

'Shall we go downstairs again?'

Stiffly, tense with nerves, she passed him as he held open the door, and almost held her breath as her shoulder brushed his chest.

Back down in the hall, Dominick leaned on the edge of the huge square oak table, lovingly polished over the centuries, and regarded her with detached speculation.

'Subject to your references confirming you're not a potential burglar or cunning art thief, when did you say you could start, Miss Stuart?'

She thought rapidly. She'd been doing temporary work as a clerical assistant in a county archives office while she waited for an opportunity to make proper use of her post-graduate diploma. She'd have to pay a month's rent on her bedsit, but at the salary being offered here that wouldn't present a problem.

'I...I could probably start a week on Monday.'

He looked unimpressed.

'Is that the earliest?'

'What did you expect? That I'd be able to start tomorrow?' she retorted, with some spirit.

He considered her with a smoulder of amusement.

'Are you always this...abrasive, Miss Emma Stuart?'

'I'm sorry. I didn't intend to sound...rude.'

'That's better. I like my employees humble, Miss Stuart. Remember that.'

It was difficult to tell if this was his quirky sense of humour talking, or if he actually meant it. Her smile was saccharine-sweet.

'Oh, I will, Mr Fleetwood.'

'Then a week on Monday it is,' he agreed, with an air of finality. He glanced at a slim Rolex on his dusky wrist, and Emma felt dismissed. 'Mrs Shields will be here to let you in, if I'm tied up in court. Make yourself at home.'

He held out his hand, and she put her own into it with a ridiculous tremor of apprehension.

'But don't use up all the hot water on a Friday night,' he added, with a wicked gleam in his eyes. 'See you, Miss Stuart...'

Emma escaped into the crunchy gravel sweep of the drive, and dived into her red Renault 5. His hand had seemed to burn her. She was trembling all over. A strong sense of panic was invading every inch of her body.

It wasn't too late, she told herself desperately as she pressed her foot on the accelerator and left the manor behind. She could still ring and say she didn't want the job. She could still get herself out of this, before she was in too deep to think straight...

But she *did* want the job, she realised in dismay. She wanted the job more than she'd ever wanted anything.

When she'd heard that Fleetwood Manor needed an archivist, her first reaction had been one of bitter curiosity, an urgent need to go and see for herself where Sir Robert Fleetwood had wrecked her parents' lives...

Now all she seemed to be able to think of was the thrill of those ancient documents awaiting discovery in the Fleetwood attics. And Dominick Fleetwood's mesmerising blue gaze.

She felt angry with herself, and frightened and bewildered by her reaction to the man she'd just met.

And she felt more alone, and more confused than ever... because how, in the name of God, could she feel such a *frisson* of awareness, such an unmistakable shiver of desire, towards a man who could well be her half-brother...?

CHAPTER TWO

EMMA swung her reading glasses off and laid them carefully on the desk, beside the faded parchment. She rubbed a grubby hand shakily over her face. She was tired, hungry, stiff with sitting for so long. The attic room was cold. It felt like the cold of centuries of unheated stone, and the small Calor-gas fire flickering beside her hadn't a hope of dispelling it. And yet inside her excitement warmed her, burned like a secret flame... She felt a consuming urgency to continue working. End of daylight spelled end of work, and she was so engrossed she didn't want to finish yet...

She caught her breath sharply, struck by the complexity of her present situation. Here she was, poring over ancient papers in the dusty, ghost-filled attics of Fleetwood Manor, deciphering letters to Sir George Fleetwood, written over four hundred years ago, back in the sixteenth century. The old iron casks and wooden boxes overflowed with a treasure-trove of historical detail...

And judging from the faded ink and parchment, Sir George's character bore lamentable similarities to his more recent descendants. Sir Robert, Dominick's father, could have been an uncanny reincarnation of his reprehensible ancestors. And Dominick...? She shivered a little. Remembering the lazy, speculative gleam in his eyes at their last encounter gave her the distinct impression that family traits lived on in the present generation...

A footstep at the door made her swivel round quickly. She'd expected to see Jamie, Mrs Shields' grandson. But Dominick Fleetwood stood there. Her stomach lurched alarmingly.

'Still at it?' He checked a slim gold watch on his wrist, and tilted a wry smile at her. 'Isn't this beyond the call of duty?'

She stood up slowly. She suddenly felt conscious of her appearance. She hadn't seen Dominick for the entire fortnight she'd been here. He hadn't come down from London last weekend. Deeply involved in her work, she'd almost forgotten that it was Friday night again, and that there was a possibility he might arrive. Now here he was, darkly devastating in dove-grey suit and charcoal silk tie, radiating aristocratic elegance, and making her feel like an unkempt maid-servant...

'It's riveting stuff,' she confessed, with a short laugh. 'I just can't stay away from it!'

'Letters and bills and inventories and rent arrears, spanning the last five and a half centuries?' he mocked softly. 'Worth starving and freezing to death over?'

Emma reached a hand up to smooth her hair. It was caught up in a thick ponytail, with strands escaping around her face, and she knew it must look a mess. Just as she must look a mess. She had pins and needles in her right foot from hooking it around the rungs of the chair for hours on end. She shook it, and stamped on it surreptitiously.

'I might be in danger of freezing, but certainly not of starving,' she retorted lightly. 'Mrs Shields and Jamie keep me supplied with a regular flow of home-made flapjacks and mugs of tea!'

'I'm glad to hear it.' She felt the cool gaze slide consideringly over her. She stiffened, her embarrassment deepening. In old jeans, a thick, baggy black polo-neck, a strawberry-pink checked shirt worn open as a jacket and clumpy Doc Marten boots she was hardly *femme fatale* material. But did she want to be? a small voice cautioned. This job, in spite of her muddled bitterness about the Fleetwood family, had proved irresistible.

It was a gem of a job. The kind every historian must surely dream about. Not just for the unique archives, but for the magnificent working environment. She'd felt deeply privileged, having the freedom to explore the old manor, admire the ancient beauty of the place. There was even a fifteenth-century Great Hall, complete with minstrels' gallery. But the idea of finding Dominick Fleetwood dangerously attractive hadn't occurred to her. It was a complication she simply hadn't considered... A sick feeling of panic crept into her stomach.

'What's wrong with your foot?'

'It's gone to sleep!' she confessed, with a grimace. 'I have this habit of twisting it round the chair when I'm sitting for a long time...'

'I told you I didn't want a Cinderella, slaving away night and day,' he rebuked softly. 'You look as if you haven't slept since you started two weeks ago!'

'Thanks a lot!' Her cheeks felt hot. How dared he make personal remarks about her appearance?

'You need some exercise,' he judged coolly. 'How do you normally keep fit?'

'I... I swim,' she heard herself saying vaguely, too taken aback by his abrupt interrogation to protest, 'and sometimes I play tennis. Or jog. But I really don't...'

'Have you got a swimming costume with you?'

'Well, yes, but I really...'

'Tennis racket?'

'No! And honestly, I...' She was reeling under his patronising directness.

'There's a place I use when I'm down in this part of the world. I was planning to spend the evening there anyway.' He shot her a sudden grin which seemed to stop her heartbeat for a few seconds. 'Stress mounts up in my business. I tend to need a lot of unwinding. Come with me. It'll do you good.'

'Oh, no, I couldn't possibly...'

'I'm not asking you, Miss Stuart,' he cut in calmly, 'I'm telling you. Rules of the job. A fit body produces an alert brain.'

'Of all the pompous...' She bit her lip on the outburst, but not before she'd seen the steely flash of amusement in his eyes.

'Careful, Miss Stuart. What happened to humility?' The narrowed gaze raked her mercilessly. She began to tingle, from her neck to her knees, where his eyes slid over her.

'Sorry, *sir*, she fenced, with mock-deference. Sketching a rough curtsy, she added with overdone meekness, 'I'll go and get ready *right* away! What would you recommend I wear?'

'Something suitable for dinner.' He nodded with bleak amusement. 'We might as well have a meal there later. I'll see you in my study in half an hour.'

This sounded horribly ominous. But she seemed to have little option. There was a warning note in the cool drawl which brought the colour surging into her face.

'All right.' She spoke through clenched teeth, but she wished her heart would stop its dull thudding against her breastbone.

Seething with resentment, she retreated to her bedroom to get ready. In her head she called him every name she could think of, to vent her feelings. Of all the autocratic, arrogant, self-opinionated, overbearing, cranky fitness freaks, he took the honours... Who did he think he was? Being temporary lord of the manor was one thing. Treating her like a half-witted child was quite another...

But the really infuriating thing, she acknowledged truthfully, was that the thought of swimming or playing tennis with Dominick Fleetwood, and then having dinner with him, secretly filled her with such conflicting feelings of dread and excitement that she trembled at the prospect of her own weakness...

Her feelings of hostility were her only protection. It was a good thing she disliked him so intensely. Because in every other respect her relationship with her employer, she reflected impatiently, seemed to be veering hopelessly off course...

The place Dominick frequented when he came down to Fleetwood Manor turned out to be an extremely exclusive country club. Immaculately landscaped grounds spread out, thickly wooded, revealing an outdoor swimming-pool, still under its winter wraps, as well as a big, covered indoor pool, and all-weather tennis courts with brand-new surfaces gleaming emerald beneath efficient floodlighting. She glanced at him apprehensively, as he drove between ranks of Rolls and Bentleys and Mercedes, and swung his forest-green Porsche into a parking place near the entrance.

'You could have warned me it was like this,' she said ruefully. 'I'm hardly in this sort of league...!'

He turned a gaze of genuine surprise on her.

'This sort of league?' he echoed calmly. 'What do you mean?'

'You must know what I mean!' She glanced down at the simple, ethnic-style full skirt she wore over a long-sleeved white body. 'Are we supposed to be having dinner here?'

'If you're worried about the way you look,' he said after a few moments' cool consideration, 'there's no need.' The smoky blue gaze assessed her clear, make-up-free skin, shiny chestnut hair and the soft curves of her figure beneath the clinging white top as he spoke. His eyes lingered fleetingly on her full breasts, nipples suddenly hard as cherry stones under his gaze. Emma felt her insides fold up in an alarming fashion, almost squeezing the breath from her lungs. Her thighs felt boneless.

'You look fine.' The verdict was succinct. He got out, retrieved their sports bags from the boot, and sent her a smile which flipped her heart over as he gestured towards the canopied entrance. In dark blue silk shirt and designer-cut charcoal trousers, he looked lean, broad-shouldered, and overwhelmingly gorgeous. The tug of attraction was so fierce, she found herself gritting her teeth . . .

It was surprisingly enjoyable, playing tennis on the floodlit outside courts. And somehow, faced with the challenge of holding her own against a player not only vastly more experienced but vastly stronger, she managed to acquit herself quite well. Dominick won, but she actually took a couple of games off him. The tingle of pleasure made her glow all over.

But one set was definitely enough. Her green tracksuit, the only suitable clothing she'd unearthed for the event, felt too warm. She wished she'd brought white skirt and T-shirt. Dominick had started in a black tracksuit, but discarded the trousers after the first couple of games, revealing white shorts and long, healthily tanned legs, coarsely haired and with impressively honed muscles.

'You play quite well,' he complimented her. He met her at the net and wryly observed her pink cheeks and air of triumphant enjoyment. 'Do you want to play the best of three?'

She shook her head. 'Are you trying to kill me off? I got to a reasonable standard when I was at school, but I'm so out of practice I'm amazed I managed to win any games at all!'

'You won them fairly,' he assured her. 'All I held back on was my serve.'

'Just as well!' The power of Dominick's returns had been sufficient evidence of the potential velocity of his normal service. She blew upwards to lift the damp strands of her hair from her forehead, and shot him a tentative smile. 'I'm roasting in this tracksuit. Can we have a swim now?'

'Indeed we can, Miss Stuart.' The gleam in the blue eyes was difficult to gauge. But the heat from playing tennis seemed to intensify into another kind of heat as she felt his eyes rake assessingly over her figure beneath the green jersey of the tracksuit.

It took only minutes to swap tracksuit for swimsuit, and the water felt deliciously refreshing as she slid in. She glanced warily round for Dominick. He'd appeared at the deep end, dark and intensely masculine in brief navy swimming trunks. She watched, transfixed, as he paused, then dived cleanly in with an impressive ripple of muscle. Her steady breaststroke seemed rather feeble compared with his several lengths of masterly front crawl. He finally surfaced a few feet in front of her, laughing.

'Feeling better?'

'Yes,' she admitted, trying not to react to the threat of his nearness. 'Yes, thanks. Much better. I always do when I get around to exercising . . .'

'You look better already,' he assured her. 'You've lost that pinched, tense look, Miss Stuart. It suits you.'

'Thank you, Mr Fleetwood.'

'Come on, we'll finish with a Jacuzzi.' Swimming easily to the side, he swung himself out on to the tiles, and reached down to catch hold of her arm, pulling her out beside him. The intimate contact was almost too much to bear. Finding herself standing next to him on the side of the pool, clad only in the clinging wet fabric of her black costume, felt as compromising as standing naked with a stranger . . .

'You're shivering,' he observed, eyeing the goosebumps which had sprung to the surface of her skin. 'Are you cold again already?'

He was steering her towards the Jacuzzi in the corner of the pool, his fingers warmly confident on her wet skin.

'No. I'm not cold exactly... it's... it's just the contrast... and actually I've never been in a Jacuzzi...' She was babbling nervously, she realised, annoyed with herself.

'The Jacuzzi is hot.' He dropped a coin into the slot and gestured into the foaming oval. Hesitating, she stood motionless on the edge as he stepped down into it, sat down and stretched his long, dark body across the width. 'Come along, Miss Stuart. A new relaxation experience awaits you...'

Could she face joining him in what looked like an unbearably small and intimate space? Dragging air into strained lungs, she forced her wayward emotions under control. She was behaving like a prudish schoolgirl. There were plenty of other people swimming near by. He could be her *brother*, she reminded herself fiercely. Whatever this stupid shimmer of awareness signified, it certainly couldn't come to anything. Sheer moral will-power would see to that... And the longer she stood here, with his lidded gaze humorously assessing her hesitation, the longer her body was exposed to that enigmatic male scrutiny...

She put one foot down into the bubbling water. The warmth was bliss after the cool of the swimming-pool. But the steps down were invisible, now that the water was foaming so fiercely. Taking another step in, she missed her footing. With a choked exclamation, she plunged forward. Disappearing under the surface, she burst up again to find herself sprawled ignominiously on top of Dominick. The sensation was electrifying.

'Very interesting,' he murmured teasingly, 'but would you mind keeping to your own side?' As he spoke, she felt strong hands capture her around her waist. She was lifted clear of his body. But not before the sensitive swell of her breasts had made firm contact with the coarse muscle of his chest and abdomen. And not before the slender length of her thighs had become embarrassingly entangled with the rough length of his legs.

'Sorry...' She was crimson. She could feel the acute embarrassment staining her cheeks and her neck.

'Don't be, I enjoyed it.' A gleam of laughter lurked in his eyes, but his expression was deadpan as he observed her crumbled composure without compunction. 'Miss Stuart,' he added, on a huskier, taunting drawl, 'would you just relax? Club rules are very strict on sexual antics in the Jacuzzi. I'm not about to rip your costume off and have my wicked way with you, whatever you might imagine.'

The sardonic humour flayed her bruised ego. His amusement was palpable. He was finding her excruciatingly funny, she realised furiously.

Slowly, she turned large grey eyes on him, all her buried resentment swirling to the surface, unbidden.

'I'm obviously providing tonight's entertainment,' she said stiffly. 'Was that why you insisted I come out with you this evening? Because you wanted some comic relief from your gruelling two weeks in court?'

His eyelids masked his expression as he watched her flushed face.

'What a touchy young lady you are,' he mused softly. 'And where did you get such a low opinion of yourself?'

'It's not *myself* I have the low opinion of...' The retort burst out, and she trailed off, aghast. Dominick's expression had altered slightly. The lazy amusement had changed to a cooler, more dissecting curiosity. The shrewd barrister-like penetration was back in his eyes.

'Let's get this straight—you're implying that you have a low opinion of me?'

'I...' Hopeless, she realised miserably. Even disregarding his cool arrogance at the suggestion that he could be less than perfect, how she'd ever imagined she could hide her mixed feelings, keep past resentments hidden, she'd never know...

'Well? What have I done to incur your disapproval, Miss Stuart?'

'Nothing...really, nothing...' Apart from being unbearably conceited, domineering, and sadistically *mocking*, she screamed silently. Just as she imagined his father must have been...

Overcome with panic, she stood up, and tried to wade out of the surging water. He stood up too, and steadied her as she wobbled. His warm hands on her shoulders sent shock-waves of pure, unmistakable sexual desire streaking through her nerve-ends. Choked and breathless, she made it on to the firm surface, and retrieved her towel. The big white bath-sheet had come from the manor house, and she wrapped its fluffy length around herself like a shield.

Dominick had followed her out.

'I'm going to have a hot shower,' he said casually, looping his own towel round his neck and switching subjects, to her relief. 'I recommend you do the same. I'll meet you in the bar in about half an hour.'

'Yes. Fine...'

'Oh, and just to satisfy my curiosity,' he murmured ruthlessly, catching her by the fold of her towel, where she'd fastened it tightly across her breasts, 'I'd like to try this...'

Without warning, he dropped his head and kissed her, hungrily, shockingly, on her lips. The combination of the kiss, warm, masculine and demanding, and the contact of his knuckles against the soft swell of her cleavage was terrifyingly intense. Rigid with denial, she stood like a statue, outwardly frozen. Inside, some hidden reactor went into fatal meltdown. The taste of him, the scent of his body, the teasing exploration of his tongue inside her mouth, everything conspired to demolish her defences.

It took every ounce of horrified awareness to push him away. She faced him for a fraught moment, trembling all over. The blue gaze was unrepentantly amused. Her own grey gaze was wide with fury.

'Please *don't* try it again!' she managed unsteadily. 'Or you'll be looking for a new archivist...'

Spinning angrily away, she made for the changing-rooms. Almost blindly, she stumbled to find her soap-bag, and then dived beneath the wonderfully hot showers, shampooing her hair and soaping her whole body.

She felt as if she'd somehow stepped into an impossible nightmare. She'd thought she could handle this complex situation. Now she realised it was going to be much, much harder than she'd imagined. This physical attraction to Dominick was disastrous. It was more than disastrous. It was...it was unthinkable...

She closed her eyes and let the shampoo run down her face, trying to free her mind from its turmoil. She felt hot inside. Hot, and bewildered, and full of self-disgust... If Dominick *was* her half-brother, that was bad enough. It made him scandalously out of bounds, in all normal societies... But a sense of bitter disloyalty was also stabbing through her. Behind her closed eyelids, it was images of her father that taunted her, in the months before he died.

As long as she could remember, she'd been told that the Fleetwood family had wrecked her parents' lives. That Sir Robert Fleetwood, Dominick's father, was to blame for everything that had gone so tragically wrong in her parents' marriage. And yet now here she was, being taken out by Dominick Fleetwood tonight. And as well as hating him for his cool arrogance and despising him for *who* he was she was feeling these powerful, overwhelming, swelling bursts of excitement when she was with him...

She rubbed her fingers furiously through her wet hair, rinsing out the last of the bubbles. With her eyelids squeezed shut, she felt as if she was going mad. How could she have been so stupid as to go for this job, knowing what her father had told her about the Fleetwood males?

Emerging from the shower, she wrapped herself in her towel and went to sit on the wooden bench, while she fought to make sense of her feelings...

She was angry with Dominick tonight. But it wasn't because of anything his father had done to her mother years ago. It wasn't because he was a Fleetwood. She was angry with him because he made her feel vulnerable, and gauche. And she was angry with him because that physical contact in the Jacuzzi and that taunting kiss had made her quiver inside with a melting clench of desire she'd never felt before... She had to search for the evidence to prove her father's version of the past. That was the most urgent task she had to undertake. The irony was that before meeting Dominick she'd have found a degree of vengeful satisfaction in proving that Sir Robert was her real father. Now she was so confused, she had no idea what she wanted to find out any more...

'Have you chosen?'

She glanced up from the menu to find him lazily observing her. They were having pre-dinner drinks at the bar, seated on stools. She took a shaky sip of her dry Martini, and tried to decide what she wanted to eat.

'Not...not quite.' She couldn't even concentrate on the menu. The elaborate black script on cream vellum danced and blurred in front of her eyes.

She was too aware of him, she acknowledged bleakly. He seemed far too close for comfort, even sitting a foot away on an adjacent bar stool. He smelled faintly of some expensive sandalwood aftershave. He looked very large, very male and very intimidating. Very dangerous. She felt as if her breath was restricted in her chest.

'You're very...quiet, Miss Stuart,' he commented idly after another silence had elongated. 'Are you always so tense? Or are you frightened of me?'

She looked up from the menu warily.

'Of course I'm not frightened of you.' She hoped she sounded convincing to him, because she didn't to herself.

'Aren't you?' The taunting blue gaze examined her face, observing the changes of expression. She felt her temper beginning to fray.

'We hardly know each other. And we... we're hardly on the same social circuit! I'm just an employee! Do you expect me to chatter away like an old friend?' She'd meant to snap the words with cool precision, but instead they came out shakily, even defensively.

Beneath the soft white jersey of her clinging body, she felt her skin beginning to heat nervously. Dominick's amused gaze slid to her throat, and flicked lower, to the revealing scoop-necked design of her bodice, where the swell of her breasts was clearly visible. Quelling her agitation, she lifted her hand to finger the small silver locket at her neck. There was a picture of her mother inside it. Dad had given it to her, just before he died...

'I was intrigued by the idea that you hold a low opinion of me, Miss Stuart.'

You would be, she thought ruefully, having such a high opinion of yourself...

'I hardly know you,' she heard herself repeating woodenly. 'What possible reason could I have for feeling that way?'

'That's what interests me...' His eyes were lidded, difficult to read. Calmly changing the subject, he added, 'If you're feeling indecisive, I recommend the scallops in white wine sauce followed by the pheasant in Madeira. Or are you vegetarian?'

'No...' She swallowed her pride, gave up on the menu. After toying briefly with the idea of refusing his suggestion, she nodded stiffly. 'That sounds fine.'

'Good . . .' An almost undiscernible flick of his hand brought the head waiter and the wine waiter hurrying to his side. Her heart still pumping much faster than it should, she listened as he calmly gave their order, chose a Muscadet and a Médoc to complement each course, then turned his attention back to focus on her with that unsettling intensity.

Emma chewed her lip. Her mouth tasted of the dusky pink lip-gloss she'd applied after her shower, aiming at a little more poise and sophistication. She'd wanted to be cool and chic, more than a match for this man's dangerous masculine charm. But, catching sight of herself in the huge gilt-edged mirror above the bright log fire opposite the bar, she saw with a sinking heart that her neat chignon was collapsing slightly on top, tendrils of glossy dark chestnut cascading from the silver clip.

Her cheeks looked flushed, her grey eyes, slightly myopic, looking enormous in the small oval of her face. The opulence of their setting didn't help. All around there were poised and confident women, wearing priceless designer dresses and flirting elegantly with suave and wealthy men. And there she was, looking as flushed and uncertain as a shy sixth-former on her first dinner date.

'So for the past fortnight you've been beavering away in the attics, poring over old papers?'

'More or less, yes. Mrs Shields and Jamie have kept me well supplied with food and drinks. And Jamie has helped with any heavy lifting...'

'Jamie's a good lad,' Dominick agreed coolly. 'I'm surprised he hasn't done more with his life than odd jobs around the estate for my father.'

'There's nothing wrong with choosing a practical career, if that's what you want,' she countered quickly. 'My father was bored rigid by office work. He loved being out of doors. He didn't mind the low pay. He had his freedom...'

'Are your parents still alive?'

'No. They're both dead.' She saw his enquiring expression, and felt compelled to expand.

'My parents were separated. I lived with my mother until she was killed in a road accident five years ago. Then I went to live with my father. He developed bronchial pneumonia. He died last year.'

'That must have been hard for you. Do you have any other relatives?' Dominick's tone was a lazy, casual drawl. But his gaze was searching, disturbing her with its concentration.

Emma shook her head. The irony of this conversation was almost too much to contend with.

'So at the tender age of twenty-two there's just you? No one else at all?'

'You make me sound like a...a poor little orphaned child, or something!'

'Isn't that exactly what you are? Except that I can see you're an adult.' Dominick gave a slight smile. 'A very composed young adult, with a lot of suppressed emotion simmering under the surface. Would it help if I apologised for embarrassing you in the Jacuzzi, Miss Stuart?'

The heat coursed up into her neck and cheeks, and she clenched her hands furiously in her lap.

'There's no need to apologise for that. It was my fault. It was I who...who slipped—but it might help if you apologised for kissing me afterwards!'

His gaze had narrowed, the gleam of amusement more discernible.

'Miss Stuart...may I call you Emma?'

'I...I suppose you can. You *are* my...my boss!'

'All right. Emma. I apologise. It was an impulse, and I'm sorry if it upset you. Now will you relax?' He was mocking her, she knew. And yet there was something powerfully compelling about his curt instruction. Relax? If she relaxed too much, she'd be too vulnerable. Confusion rocked her forcefully. She felt like a ship adrift in cross-currents.

'I...' She found she was holding her breath. Abruptly, she expelled it. She managed a slight, wary smile. 'I am relaxed. Perfectly relaxed.'

The dark blue gaze held hers, then he gave a short laugh.

'You are? This is progress. Tell me how the research is coming on.'

This, at least, represented relatively safe waters. She outlined her progress so far. She told him about the incriminating evidence of the heart-breaking letter to the sixteenth-century Sir George Fleetwood from what appeared to be his children's governess.

'He was a wicked womaniser,' Dominick agreed, without a flicker of reflected shame, 'but he had some redeeming aspects. I believe he used to risk his life by hiding recusant priests from imprisonment or execution...'

'Did he?'

Dominick nodded, his lips twisting. 'So the legend has it. There are two secret hiding places, small compartments, in the south-west turret,' he added calmly, 'between the newel staircase and a space in the floor of the top turret room. They were discovered in the nineteenth century...'

'*Really*?' Emma, complicated resentments forgotten, felt her eyes glowing with anticipation.

'They were revealed during some renovation work, complete with palliasse bed, folding leather altar, and a few rather less pleasant relics...'

Emma gripped her hands together excitedly. 'Can I see them?'

He inclined his hand, his eyes wry.

'Of course. Although the *bones* were given a decent Christian burial, I believe.'

'Bones?' Her grey eyes widened in horror. She suppressed a shudder. 'You don't mean someone actually died there, trapped?'

'It's all conjecture. But I imagine so, yes. Perhaps the system had a flaw—someone had to remember you were in there after the persecutors had gone.'

'How ghastly...'

'Mmm. Of course, the tales of ghostly screams floating from the south-west turret are total fabrication,' Dominick went on nonchalantly, 'just as the stories of grey shapes on the attic landing are figments of over-active imaginations...'

'You're making this up!' She was half frowning, half laughing.

Dominick's dark face was deadpan.

'Yes. But at least it made you laugh. You're a very... intense young lady, Emma...'

'Dominick!' The female voice was light and amused, and Emma swivelled round to see a girl with straight blonde hair and bright red lipstick advancing on them. 'Dominick, sweetheart! What a lovely surprise!'

'Vanessa.' Dominick had risen easily to his feet, but his dark face was blandly expressionless as the girl stretched up to kiss his cheek. 'What are you doing in Warwickshire?'

'Hoping to bump into you, darling, what else?' the girl teased huskily, switching an emerald-green gaze on to Emma and lifting an eyebrow enquiringly. 'I hope I'm not interrupting anything?'

'This is Emma Stuart,' Dominick said smoothly. 'She's working for me at the manor, sorting through Fleetwood's records. Emma, this is Vanessa Buckingham. An old friend and neighbour, and a fellow lawyer.'

Emma shook hands, noting the girl's elegantly slim figure in a clinging black crêpe skirt and halter-neck top.

Vanessa had laughed at Dominick's introduction.

'Mmm. While Dominick makes the headlines with his evil cross-examination techniques in the High Court, I have to content myself with being in-house lawyer for a department store...'

Since the department store she named was famous world-wide, the self-deprecation carried little weight, Emma decided. Vanessa Buckingham was obviously a very high-powered lawyer indeed...

'I'm here with Hugo and Jan,' Vanessa was saying to Dominick. The girl's green eyes were caressing him with blatant hunger. Emma hooked her foot round the leg of her stool, and fiddled with her glass. A strange feeling seemed to be gripping her, making her feel slightly sick.

Here, she reminded herself firmly, was an example of the kind of woman Dominick normally spent his time with. Glamorous, clearly upper-class, from his own background, someone who moved in the same circles, socially and professionally. Mentally retreating from the situation, she tried to concentrate on the work she'd been doing today, to focus her mind on the real reason for being here.

'Why don't you join us?' Dominick was suggesting smoothly to Vanessa Buckingham. 'I'll tell Giuseppe we'd like a table for six.'

Emma felt her stomach clench. What was the matter with her? She should welcome this diversion with relief, shouldn't she? All she had to do was sit out the meal, making the minimum of contributions to the conversation. The heat was off...

But relief wasn't what she felt at all. Now, watching Dominick's dark face, laughing at something the blonde girl had said, and listening to their conversation about the rarefied legal world in London, she suddenly felt gauche, boring, provincial.

Worst of all, the sick sensation growing in her solar plexus was definitely an unexpected and wholly inappropriate thrust of jealousy...

CHAPTER THREE

EMMA sat in silence in the car on the way back to the manor. The powerful headlights swept past dark hedgerows and inky black woods. She stared at the arcs of light, and tried to make her mind go blank. Anything to avoid thinking about the evening she'd just spent at the country club. In fact, anything to avoid thinking at all . . .

The evening had not been a success. At least, not for Emma. She'd held her own reasonably well, she thought. Given a passably witty explanation of her job as an archivist, when graciously invited to explain her presence. But when she'd calmly stated that her father had been gamekeeper at Fleetwood Manor when she was a child, there'd been a wry exchange of glances between Dominick's three friends. Vanessa, Hugo and Jan had exuded that exclusive, cliquey rapport that came with shared childhoods, shared schooling, shared backgrounds.

And her own confidence, shaky at best, had dissolved in the knowledge that Dominick had jumped at the chance to liven up his evening by inviting them to his table.

But Dominick had seemed preoccupied throughout the meal. The seafood with its delicate sauce had been superb. And the pheasant, rich and aromatic, served with fine-cut sautéd potatoes, and perfectly cooked broccoli, mange-tout and carrots, had been mouthwatering. But she'd felt rather too on edge to relax fully and enjoy the country club's excellent cuisine. Infuriatingly, she'd found she was drawn, constantly, to look at Dominick as he leaned back in his chair, long brown fingers idly twisting the stem of his wine glass, shuttered gaze surveying the gathered company with cool disinterest. He'd kept his contributions to the conversation brief and sparingly to the point. His dark blue eyes, shadowed in the candlelight at their table, had been unreadable.

And once or twice, as she sat and listened to the high-spirited conversation between the other three, she'd found him looking at her. The sensation had been disturbing. And when their eyes had met she'd felt that fluttery tension in her stomach all over again.

'Did you enjoy your evening?' The casual query was directed at her as they emerged from the long, wooded drive to the manor and swept to a halt by the imposing entrance. In the glow of the coachlight by the vast, studded wooden doors, he switched off the ignition and turned to examine her face, his eyes lidded.

'Yes. Thank you.' The polite reply held little enthusiasm. She felt impatient with herself. How ungracious, she scolded herself silently.

'You don't sound as if you did,' he pointed out, with calm curiosity. 'You're a very self-contained young lady, Emma. There's something unnerving about your... nun-like gravity.' The teasing was relentless.

'I'm sorry if I've bored you so much,' she retorted frostily. Her heart was thumping faster. Fumbling for the door-handle, she went very still as Dominick put out a hand and restrained her. His fingers were light on her upper arm, but the casual physical contact seemed to pierce her with dozens of unwanted reactions.

'You don't bore me at all,' he assured her evenly. 'You interest me.'

'Mr Fleetwood...'

'Dominick,' he advised briefly. He took his hand away from her arm. She felt as if a hole had been burned there. Suddenly there didn't seem to be any air in the car. Her breasts rose and fell jerkily as her breathing became more erratic.

'Emma...' The deep voice held a note of impatient amusement. He caught her chin in his fingers, and twisted her hot face round to inspect her expression. 'What exactly is going through that secretive little head of yours?'

'Secretive...?' Her voice was huskily indignant. The thump of her heart had become a pounding. 'I've no idea what you're talking about...!'

'I'm not a complete fool,' he murmured, eyeing her parted lips with a darkening gaze, 'and I'm well-trained at detecting hidden undercurrents. This evening has been laden with them. You're hiding something, my sweet little Emma. I don't know what your story is yet, but I fully intend to find out.'

'Let go of me...' It was a strained whisper. Every pore in her body seemed to be shuddering with sensual need.

'Will you calm down?' He dropped his hand from her chin. There was an insulting note of humour in his voice.

'There are laws against this kind of...of sexual harassment of employees...'

'Sexual?' His echo was blandly mocking. 'Is that what you think this evening has been about? Sexual harassment?' Dominick's face was shadowy in the semi-darkness. But she could see it well enough to read the incredulous amusement.

'Don't patronise me, please!' Her angry retort came without premeditation. She hadn't realised quite how furious she was, until his soft goad. Quite why she felt so incensed she wasn't sure. A combination of things. The awkwardness of the evening. Her guilt at finding him so attractive. Fear at the current swirl of sensual temptation, sitting so close to his overtly masculine form, in the darkness of the car's interior...

'Is that why you've been looking at me as if I were a cross between Count Dracula and Casanova all evening? Did you think I was so desperate for female company, I was softening you up with dinner before visiting you in your bed tonight?'

'You tell me!'

Her conflicting responses were clearly communicating themselves to him, because with a thin twist of his lips he reacted by moving a few inches closer, slipping one hand loosely around the back of her neck, and fingering the sensitive hollow of her nape.

'All right, I'll tell you. I don't think you know what you want. But I think you want...something.' The cruel mockery was like a physical assault. But his touch, his fingers in her hair, was raising her temperature, pounding through her system.

'Please...' Her voice was strained. Like someone's else's voice. A stranger's voice. 'Don't...don't touch me...'

'Don't you want me to touch you?' Dominick sounded different, too. He still looked amused, but his deep voice had thickened slightly. His smoky blue gaze had narrowed, focused on her parted lips. She could almost feel a tingle in the place where his eyes were trained.

She felt helplessly angry. Not with Dominick, more with herself. Taking this job had been stupid. Ill-advised. Immature. Her feelings were too irrational. Finding this flare of attraction to Dominick Fleetwood was a blow she hadn't foreseen. A tornado of conflicting emotions was spinning inside her head.

'Since you raised the subject of sex, I admit I do find you attractive, Emma.' The husky, thoughtful taunt made her freeze in her seat. She could hardly breathe. His fingers stroked round the slender column of her throat, and moved lightly down the swell of her breasts at the scoop neck of her top, following the indent of her slight cleavage. He took the silver locket in his hand and rubbed it gently with his thumb.

She was quivering all over. The softness of her breasts seemed to swell at the warm nearness of his knuckles. Part of her screamed for him to stop, another seemed silently to beg him to move his hand sideways, to spread the palm wide and touch the tingling, tender jut of her breasts, caress the tight ache of her nipples. She gasped involuntarily and caught his hand furiously, protecting herself with her arms.

'Stop it . . .' she whispered, her voice choked. He ignored her.

'In fact, I find you sexually attractive . . .' With leisurely ease, he caught hold of both her hands and pushed them down to her sides, exposing her to his view. His touch was hard, warm and dry against her wrists. He let his dark gaze move slowly up and down her body, reducing her bones to jelly. She opened her mouth to hurl a protest at him, but no sound came out.

'There's *definitely* something about you,' he continued tauntingly. 'The way your mouth curves, the shape of your breasts and hips . . .

Frankly, Miss Emma Stuart, I freely confess that I'd rather like to...'

The drawled words he used were coolly, lazily, shockingly explicit. She began to shiver convulsively all over. Heat flooded her face. In spite of her humiliation, her breasts tingled. She felt her nipples tug and pull harder beneath the smooth fabric of the white top. The knowledge that he was looking at her body, that he was coolly observing her arousal, made her stomach hollow alarmingly.

'If you think I'm interested in...in casual sex with you, you're crazy...' she hissed painfully. Even if he had no idea that they might share a father, how *dared* he treat her like some cheap little sex object?

'There'd be nothing casual about it, if I took you to bed with me,' he growled softly. 'But I suppose you're expecting me to apologise?'

His expression gave away nothing of his real mood, but she thought his dark face looked gaunt and predatory. For the first time she felt a small shiver of real, raw fear trickle down her spine. Apart from Mrs Shields, and her grandson Jamie, who slept a long way away from the habitable bedrooms on the first floor, she was completely alone tonight with Dominick Fleetwood, with no idea how she was going to handle this potentially explosive attraction she felt towards him...

'No, I'm not,' she ground out unsteadily. 'I'm quite sure you're not the kind of man who apologises for anything!'

'But how can you know what kind of man I am?'

'Actions speak louder than words,' she heard herself retort, her voice tight. 'If... if you were a *gentleman*, you wouldn't have spoken to me the way you just did!' Heavens, she sounded like a prudish little Victorian governess, she thought dimly. No wonder he found her so hilariously entertaining...

'I stand firmly rebuked, Emma. And I do apologise,' he murmured, with tautly suppressed humour. 'I had no right to give in to temptation, to speak so... frankly to a young lady in my employ. Am I forgiven?'

'I...'

She stopped abruptly as Mrs Shields emerged from the entrance. The housekeeper bustled over to the car. Casting Emma a brief, smouldering grin, Dominick unhurriedly opened his door and stepped out.

'Thank goodness you're back, Mr Dominick,' Mrs Shields began without prevarication. 'A solicitor rang from London. There's some news for you. About Mr Richard. The gentleman said you could ring him back tonight—he left a private number...'

Emma scrambled out of the passenger seat and came around to join them as they walked into the lamp-lit hall. Flushed and shaky, and still quivering with nerves, she made for the stairs. Dominick called her back.

'Come into the study for a moment, Miss Stuart.' The warning note in his voice indicated that she'd be wise to obey. 'You're sorting out this family's past. You may as well be a witness to developments in the present.'

Stubbornly, conscious of Mrs Shield's presence as a kind of protection, she shook her head.

'The past has little relevance to the present in this case,' she managed hoarsely. 'If...if you'll excuse me, I'm rather tired. I'm going to bed...'

She'd annoyed him, she registered, with a fleeting shiver of dismay. Turning quickly, she fled up the stairs. Too late now to question the wisdom of provoking him to fresh anger. Too late to wonder what Mrs Shields had made of the little scene. All she wanted was her room, and the re-assurance of privacy, a locked door, a warm bed to curl up in...and tomorrow, archives or no archives, she was going to have to leave...

The bathroom door leading into Dominick's room had a lock. She turned the key, and tried the knob to satisfy herself. Then, stripping fast, trembling with tension and reaction to the fraught nature of the evening, she got ready for bed at high speed, hauling on her nightdress and plaiting her heavy chestnut hair, eyeing her shadowy-eyed reflection in the long mirror with a degree of resignation.

Tonight, she reflected miserably, had been a disaster. Whichever way you looked at it, it had been a complete fiasco. What was she *doing* here?

A job, she answered herself silently, climbing into bed. A job which she'd been lucky to get, and had been quite incapable of resisting. A job which she'd now have no option but to abandon...

As for her other, more woolly-minded notions—the silly notion of balancing the books against the Fleetwoods, somehow to instigate a reckoning for their crimes against her family—she was out of her depth there, she knew. She was no match for Dominick Fleetwood. He was like a black panther, smoothly dangerous, lethally attractive...

And it was all very well recoiling like a prim Victorian maiden at his masculine taunts tonight. Fine to tell herself she'd been insulted, exploited, humiliated by a lecherous, overbearing boss... But her own feelings mirrored his. All evening, she'd been quelling the urge to look at him, to touch him again the way she'd accidentally touched him in the Jacuzzi... He wasn't stupid. He'd seen the expression in her eyes, he'd picked up on the vibrations...

She was on fire inside whenever she thought about him...and his arrogantly crude suggestion in the car burned through her body, clenching her pelvic muscles and causing a meltdown of desire so wanton that she almost moaned aloud...

But the Fleetwood males were all the same, she reminded herself despairingly. Presumably her mother had succumbed to Sir Robert's advance without too much force? It must run in the family, more strongly than she could have foreseen. The danger lay in the total lack of conscience. The thrill of the chase was all that mattered. Commitment was a dirty word to the Fleetwoods... and as for *arrogance*...

She tossed and turned, feverish with confusion. The bed was wonderfully comfortable—it felt like a real feather-bed—but sleep seemed a million miles away. When she heard an abrupt knocking on her bedroom door, she stiffened, and sat up. Clicking on the beside lamp and grabbing her watch, she checked the time.

It was midnight, she registered dimly. It felt like the early hours.

'Who is it?'

'Dominick.'

A fresh wave of heat prickled the surface of her skin, all over. Panic engulfed her. Of all the nerve...! To come to her bedroom, presumably to claim the same *droit de seigneur* as Sir Robert had with her mother... In a trembling voice she said, 'What do you want?'

'To get into the bathroom.' The curt note took her by surprise. He didn't sound particularly persuasive, or... seductive...

'To *what*?'

'Emma, will you just open this door?'

Slowly, reluctantly, she swung herself out of bed and ran barefoot across the polished boards of the floor. Unlocking her door, she peered suspiciously out into the landing. Dominick stood there, wearing a dark green and navy striped towelling dressing-gown. He had a large white towel slung over his shoulder. A fierce shadow of stubble darkened his lower jaw. He looked so lean and male and darkly sensual that she felt her insides turn to water.

'Is this some kind of joke?' she whispered furiously.

'If it is, it's on me,' he retorted bluntly. 'You've locked my connecting door to the bathroom.'

'Oh...!' She rubbed her eyes wearily. 'But you could have asked me to unlock it for you, on my side...'

'I'll do that. You can get back into bed.' He raked her appearance with a lazy masculine gaze, taking in the long, old-fashioned white cotton nightgown, pin-tucked and button-fronted, the thick dark plait down her back. 'Sorry if I woke you.'

'You didn't.' She retreated quickly to bed and retired beneath the covers, shivering, even though she wasn't cold.

Dominick strode through to the bathroom and slammed and locked the door. It was a heavy, solid door, and she heard no further sound until at least ten minutes had passed. Then, just as abruptly, he unlocked her bathroom door and came back into her room.

'Don't tell me, the key's stuck?' she demanded indignantly. 'You've decided you'll have to use my bedroom as permanent access to the bathroom?'

'No. I came to see if you want me to lock your bedroom door for you before I go through to my room.'

'That's OK. I'll do that myself when you've gone.'

'This is a crazy arrangement.' He grinned slightly. But the grin didn't quite reach his eyes, she decided, looking at him nervously. He looked...distraught. The telephone call to London, perhaps?

'Is...is everything all right?' she ventured huskily. 'Have they traced your brother?'

'Oh, yes, they've traced him.' The reserved note held a layer of anger, or was it bitterness?

'So he'll be back soon?'

'No...' With a jerky, tired gesture, he raked his hand through the thick black curls of his hair. She stared at him, suddenly realising how bleak he looked. Not just bleak, haggard.

'My brother died. Over a year ago. In the Tibetan mountains. Nobody knew who he was, so the family wasn't told.'

She sat up in bed. The pity stabbing through her was tinged with a ridiculous desire to offer him some kind of comfort.

'But...that's terrible. I'm so sorry...'

'Yeah...' He raked a hand over his face, and grimaced. 'Me too.'

'Will...will you go out there? Bring the body home...?'

'I think not. Richard died where he wanted to be. At a Tibetan monastery. He'd become a devout Buddhist, so the story goes.' There was a world-weary cynicism in his voice. 'I don't think he'd thank us for exhuming him and returning him to Church of England soil. Do you?'

'No. No...perhaps not...' Her eyes met his. Warm grey and smoky blue locked together for a long, wordless moment.

'I'm so sorry...' she repeated helplessly.

He came to sit on the side of her bed. At closer quarters, his black hair looked damp. He smelled clean and masculine, faintly of soap, and a fresh minty waft of toothpaste. There was a longish pause while they gazed at each other. Then the pause lengthened into a weighty silence. She felt trapped in the depths of his gaze.

'Do you have any idea how seductive you look in that Victorian governess nightdress?' he demanded huskily.

'I didn't *invite* you into my bedroom...' Her senses were beginning to fray and unravel at the edges. Her throat was dry.

'I should think not,' he taunted softly. He reached to take hold of her hand, pulling it towards him. She swallowed jerkily.

He turned her hand over and examined the soft underside with lidded eyes. The palm stretched out for inspection was smooth, the linear channels finely marked, the pad of flesh at the thumb joint plump and unlined. 'Prim and proper Miss Emma Stuart wouldn't dream of such unseemly behaviour...'

Slowly, he let go of her hand. Her fingers tingled where he'd touched her. In spite of his cool taunt, he looked so gaunt and miserable, her heart seemed to swell with an emotion she couldn't name.

'Mr Fleetwood...' She was in turmoil. Every sensible pore in her body was resisting this crazy urge to make closer contact. And yet her heart was hammering, her senses were spiralling into hot confusion. 'Dominick...'

Her soft, despairing use of his first name made him jerk a narrowed, darker gaze up at her face. Almost of its own volition, her hand reached to touch his hand, squeezing the supple length of his fingers.

'Dominick?' he mocked unevenly. 'It's *Sir* Dominick now, my dear Miss Stuart...'

But as he spoke he was pulling her forward into his arms and cradling her hard against his chest. And even as his sardonic words sank in the physical effect of his closeness lit an instant conflagration. Snatching in a sharp, agonised breath, she wrapped shaky arms round his neck. It was no use. She might dislike him intensely, resent him for his sarcastic arrogance, fear the unthinkable fact that they could be related... but some deeper emotion rashly dismissed all that and drove her, shivering, closer against him. The need was too great, on some dark, powerful level she'd never encountered before. She closed her eyes and gave in to the urgent need to hold him, to be held by him...

For a few moments he crushed her to his chest, his face in the scented silk of her hair. She could feel his heart thudding evenly against her own erratic beat.

Prising her away again, he raked her with darkening eyes. Without thinking, by her instinctive reaction to him, she'd awakened something primitive between them, something which took no account of their real relationship. Something which discounted the fact that they were virtual strangers. He slowly lifted his hand and began to undo the buttons at the neck of her nightdress.

Panic consumed her. But she was motionless, frozen into stillness, like a small animal caught in powerful lights. She was breathing so raggedly, the buttons were quivering as he unfastened them. The first three were released, and then he pulled the pin-tucked bodice open with abrupt impatience. Automatically she snatched her hands up to cover herself, but he caught her wrists, pulled them away, and narrowed his gaze on her.

Her naked breasts rose full, firm and pale above the white cotton. Their tips were swollen, crimson with desire. His eyes smoky with sexual hunger, Dominick trailed an exploratory finger around one rosy aureola, rotated his thumb against one flowering nipple. She heard herself give a small, husky whimper in the back of her throat. Pushing her back against the pillows, he abruptly lowered his dark head, and let his mouth explore where his finger had touched.

The shock of his mouth against her heated flesh was electrifying. It was like nothing she'd ever experienced. A pleasure and a pain rolled into one, shafting through her whole body from that one small point of contact. The sensation was so miraculous, so unexpectedly blissful, she began to tremble even harder. Raking her fingers into the thick blackness of his hair, she caught his head closer. She was hardly aware of the wanton provocation. As if in a dream, she wriggled beneath his lips, with a choked gasp of emotion.

With a rough curse, Dominick lifted his head. Then he slipped his hands beneath her armpits and pushed the generous curves of her breasts together and cupped them hard with his fingers, his eyes dark with a dangerous gleam of hunger. The hunger echoed her own, but his muttered oath had shattered the taut web he'd been spinning around her.

She tensed slightly, abruptly conscious of her dreamy surrender. With careful precision, he pulled the bodice of her nightdress over her exposed breasts. He shook his head abruptly as if he was trying to clear his brain.

'You're like a delectable little feast, waiting to be consumed,' he murmured huskily, 'but, chivalrous soul that I am, I'll dredge up the remains of my self-control.'

Her fingers felt numb as she fumbled to fasten the buttons of her nightdress. His abrupt withdrawal felt like lucky escape and cruel rejection. The contrasting reactions made her head spin.

'Chivalrous?' she managed, on a choked echo. Her face burned as humiliation caught up with her. 'About as chivalrous as...as a *highwayman*!'

Dominick's narrowed eyes had darkened to a dusky Prussian blue. He reached a lazy hand to smooth tendrils of chestnut hair from her face, his mouth wry.

'That's no way to speak to the new twelfth baronet, Sir Dominick Fleetwood, Miss Stuart.'

'I doubt if inheriting your family title will make any difference,' she whispered angrily, jerking her face away from his fingers. Regret at her stupidity was crushing her with embarrassment. 'You considered yourself God's gift to women when you were plain Dominick Fleetwood QC.'

'Your low opinion of me seems to be resurrecting itself again,' he commented, eyeing her with a deadpan air. 'But if you feel such aversion to me, why the sexual favours? If I hadn't stopped just now, how far would you have gone, Emma?'

Heat rushed into her face. His cool question hit her, like a solid missile. Anguished and despairing, she closed her eyes in mounting panic, bordering on hysteria. How far *would* she have gone? She felt sick just thinking about it. Was this physical magnetism so powerful it would have overridden all sense of decency? All social taboos?

Bitter anger came to her defence. Furious, she glared at him, hugging her arms round herself.

'You're twisting what happened! I had no idea when I ... I mean, I just felt ... sorry ...'

'*Sorry*?' His reaction was softly incredulous. 'You're saying you let things get that far because you felt sorry for me?'

'I know how it feels to lose someone you love,' she whispered tightly, 'how ... how it feels to be alive when someone close to you has died ...'

'I see.' His response was quietly assessing. After a pause, he said, 'And how does that feel, Emma?'

'As if ... as if you want to grab life with both hands and take whatever's on offer.'

He considered this in silence. His eyes held hers, observing her flushed cheeks and trembling hands with an air of cool detachment.

'Whatever the consequences?' His deep voice held an edge to it she couldn't decipher. 'Maybe you're right. Or maybe you're one very mixed-up young lady ...'

He gave her a final, penetrating gaze before he stood up abruptly. 'I think, on balance, I'd go for the latter analysis,' he added drily, heading for the connecting door. 'Goodnight, Emma. Sweet dreams ...'

CHAPTER FOUR

BREAKFAST when Dominick was at Fleetwood Manor, was a very different affair from the toast and coffee in the Aga-warmed kitchen, with Mrs Shields and Jamie. Emma made this discovery when she ventured downstairs just before nine, poked her nose round the kitchen door, and was directed to the breakfast-room, to eat 'with Mr Dominick'.

'But I only want a quick coffee and a slice of toast,' Emma began uncertainly to Mrs Shields. 'I'd planned on going straight up to the attic to sort through the work I was doing yesterday...' And to finish off neatly what she'd been in the middle of, before leaving...

'More than my life's worth,' the housekeeper declared, propelling her out of the kitchen and across the wide hall towards the breakfast-room, where the morning sun was visible in a triangle of brilliance at the open doorway. 'I was given strict instructions to direct you to the breakfast-room...'

With the greatest reluctance, last night's humiliations weighing heavy in her stomach, Emma walked into the room and faced Dominick.

He was sitting at the large oval table near the window, rifling through the pages of a large daily broadsheet.

'Good morning.' He stood up slowly as she entered. His voice held more warmth than she'd expected. And when she reached the table and sat down at the second place laid, she realised that the blue gaze appraising her appearance was not only wryly humorous but coolly appreciative. His eyes held a brilliance between the thick black lashes which sent her pulse-rate up.

He gave a twisted, self-deprecating smile. 'How did you sleep?'

Idiotically, she felt herself melt slightly inside. Dominick Fleetwood being coolly sardonic she could handle. Dominick looking at her with that lazy kindling in his eyes, Dominick being friendly and charming, Dominick oozing that laid-back sex-appeal of his felt dangerously compelling. She had the alarming feeling that it could become addictive.

'Good morning,' she echoed faintly. 'I slept all right, thanks. But I...I have to talk to you about last——'

'*Pas devant les domestiques*,' he murmured calmly. His dry tone was soft enough for her ears only, just in case the housekeeper understood any French, and knew that Emma was being warned against indiscretion in front of domestic staff. She felt her cheeks burning. She glanced round and saw Mrs Shields hovering expectantly, waiting to take her breakfast order.

'What would you like, dear?' the older woman asked encouragingly, listing an array of choices which made Emma's stomach rumble.

'I'll...I'll have a boiled egg, please. And tea...'

'And I'll have a fried egg and two rashers of bacon, please, Mrs Shields,' Dominick said smoothly, 'followed by toast and coffee.'

When they were alone, Emma stared at him in surprise.

'You weren't waiting for me, were you? Before you ordered your breakfast?'

He tilted a dark eyebrow at her.

'I thought it was the *chivalrous* thing to do,' he teased softly. 'The least I could do to make amends, after last night?'

The heat in her cheeks grew fiery. Dominick's amusement deepened. He examined her appearance, from her shiny dark hair, wound simply into a loose chignon at her nape, down to her white shirt tucked into hip-clinging blue Levis. Abruptly conscious of every nerve in her body, she hooked one booted foot nervously round the rung of her chair and fiddled with the heavy silver cutlery on the breakfast-table in front of her.

Dominick looked devastatingly attractive this morning, she registered dazedly. In well-worn blue denims and a casual, faded denim shirt, open at the neck to reveal the powerful column of his throat, his curly black hair pushed back from his face and brushing the edge of his collar, he looked not at all the way she would have expected a newly titled landowner to look. But then she

didn't know any, did she? Apart from Dominick.
And how much did she know about him? Only
that the worlds they inhabited were poles apart . . .
and that this morning he was looking at her with
a kind of reluctant, smouldering interest. Rather
like an adventurer surveying a potentially haz-
ardous conquest . . .

'So I'm allowed to talk about last night now?'
she queried softly. The flippant note didn't quite
hide her embarrassment, but she held his eyes.
'I suppose things could have been a lot worse . . .'

'Or a lot better,' he murmured drily, 'de-
pending on which way you look at it.'

His words were cool, but there was no mis-
taking the underlying masculine tease. She tensed
involuntarily. She felt vulnerable, and the feeling
deeply disturbed her. It was as if something inside
her had switched to 'self-destruct'. No good could
come of this senseless pull of attraction to
Dominick Fleetwood, she told herself miserably.
But she couldn't shake off the lingering wisps of
emotion. The longing for a replay of last night's
physical intimacy . . .

Hot in the face, she switched her gaze to study
the Fleetwood family crest on the ornately carved
oak fireplace. A lion and a lamb. And the in-
scription *Consilio et animis—more majorum—*
By wisdom and courage—after the manner of our
ancestors. The exquisite irony struck her as terribly funny. She couldn't suppress a bitter smile.

'I'll give you written notice after breakfast,' she told him quietly, turning her head to find him scrutinising her intently.

'Written notice?' His eyes hardened slightly. 'What the hell for, Emma?'

'What for? Because...because I can't continue working here...'

He expelled his breath on a long, weary sigh. The gaze he fixed on her was a mixture of impatience, disbelief and amusement.

'Because of last night?'

'What do you think?' Her heart was thudding hard under her breastbone.

'I think there's a degree of sexual attraction between us,' he said calmly. The blue eyes seemed a deeper shade of blue as they searched her hot face. 'That's not a crime, Emma.'

'Maybe not, but...'

'But you feel embarrassed,' he continued flatly. 'OK. I understand. I was at fault last night. I was feeling...frustrated. Angry with life. It was hearing about Richard's death. I thought about what you said. How it makes you feel, when someone close dies. You were right. I felt like grabbing life. Living for the moment...'

'So you grabbed me?' Her shaky half-smile brought an echoing gleam in his eyes.

'Maybe...' He grinned ruthlessly. 'Or maybe it was the other way around?'

'This is impossible!' she shot back, clenching her hands.

'Not at all. What's impossible about sexual desire?' he murmured.

In this case, everything, she wanted to shout at him. But instead she stayed silent. Last night's emotions had begun creeping up on her again, with no warning. Like a silent flood, lapping at her ankles, rising up in irresistible little waves of memory and shivers of reaction. When the sensations reached her thighs and stomach, she averted her eyes, ashamed of what he might read there.

She jumped like a frightened rabbit when he reached forward and took her hand in his. Almost transfixed, she stared down at the hard brown fingers encasing her slim palm against the contrast of the snowy white breakfast cloth. His hand was large and well-shaped. The wrist and fingers were lightly sprinkled with dark hair. The bones were finely made, the fingers strong and supple. But there was nothing visually to explain the electric shocks of reaction sparking all the way up to her neck. It took all her will-power not to return the pressure of his touch with her own fingers . . .

'Emma, whatever your problem is, it's OK,' he assured her lazily. 'I did the gentlemanly thing last night, remember?'

'If you say so.'

'Believe me, it would have been easy to let it get out of control, to take you, make love to you, do exactly what I said I'd like to do in the car,' he rasped suddenly, 'because you wanted it, and I wanted it...'

'*Please*!' Crimson flags of colour burned in her cheeks. His gaze softened a fraction as he observed her intense agitation. She tugged violently to free her hand.

'What an old-fashioned young lady you are,' he observed, releasing her hand and sitting back as the food arrived.

'And *you*,' she spat when the housekeeper had gone, 'are definitely *no* gentleman, title or no title!'

'I'm just a man,' he confirmed, with a wry grin. 'A man with a strong desire to get to know you better. I like you, Emma. I enjoy your company. Is that so... repulsive to you?'

She glanced at him, and found herself caught up, trapped in his gaze. And mesmerised by his words.

For a few seconds, wide grey eyes held in narrowed, speculative blue ones, it seemed as if all surrounding action was frozen. That even the ponderous ticking of the grandfather clock in the corner was suspended. The birdsong in the tree outside the mullioned window, the faint rattle of footsteps as someone crossed the flagstoned hall and opened the rear door, everyday noises and everyday actions, everything else seemed to be taking place on another dimension.

'Is it, Emma?' he persisted with soft insistence.

'No,' she heard herself whisper finally. She was shaking her head, without knowing how she managed to move a muscle. 'No, it's not...'

There was a wealth of charm in the slow, wry smile he directed at her.

'Then do I take it that my apology is formally accepted?'

Had he made an apology? she wondered faintly even as she nodded obediently. She felt like a puppet bidden by invisible strings.

'I suppose it had better be,' she said unevenly. Catching a life-saving gulp of air, she turned her attention exclusively on the fresh brown egg sitting in a pierced Derbyshire creamware egg-cup on the matching plate before her. Her fingers were stiff and clumsy as she slid her heavy white damask napkin from its silver ring and shook it out to cover her lap.

'Then you'll stay? Decipher those old records?'

Deeply appalled at her weakness, she could only manage a faint nod.

'Thank you, Emma.' The grave words sounded totally genuine. She found that she couldn't bring herself to glance sideways at him, to check whether that sardonic gleam had disappeared from his eyes.

'Sir George——' Dominick's hands guided her, ushering her down from the base of the rope ladder into the small, airless chamber '—used to hide the priests in here...'

'Unbelievable,' Emma breathed, gazing round her. She wasn't sure if her shortness of breath was lack of air, or the reaction to Dominick's steadying hands, which had briefly lingered on the curve of her hips.

Since breakfast, she'd spent a long time explaining to Dominick the most interesting documents in the attic, with Dominick showing such concentrated attention that she'd felt her reservations about him almost dissolving under the strength of his personality. He seemed to share her fascination with the records simply as historical evidence. In spite of everything, she was beginning to feel as if she'd known Dominick Fleetwood all her life. The sensation of familiarity, of shared tastes and an almost intimate knowledge of him, was vaguely disquieting, but even more stimulating...

'Hard to imagine how anyone could spend weeks down here,' Dominick was murmuring, eyeing the claustrophobic confines of the area. The space was no bigger than a large cupboard.

'The air is *laden* with...with atmosphere...' Emma declared dramatically, her eyes shining with fervent excitement. 'With centuries-old fear and anguish...'

'Or centuries-old dust?' The dry note in his voice made her twist to look at him. His grin was teasing.

'How prosaic!'

'My legal training versus your historical sensitivity.'

'You don't have to abandon all imagination to be a successful barrister, do you?'

'You have to work with the facts. Flights of romantic fantasy are a luxury good lawyers must do without.'

She cast him a quick, impatient look over her shoulder as she walked gingerly around the confines of the tiny hiding place.

'So you think this exonerates Sir George for his wicked mistreatment of his female staff?' she enquired. 'His willingness to risk prison or execution for harbouring recusant Catholic priests?'

'It highlights another side to his character,' Dominick suggested mildly. 'Shows the man wasn't all blackhearted chauvinism?'

'Maybe you're just touchy about your ancestors?'

He laughed softly.

'I'm the first to admit the Fleetwood males are an arrogant, self-centred bunch.'

'You speak from personal experience?'

The taunt came involuntarily, and she found herself caught by the shoulder and swivelled round to face him. In the murky light, his features looked unfamiliar, harder, darker, abruptly tinged with cruel amusement.

'Naturally...' The moment blurred as he cupped her face in his hands, and he bent to kiss her. The jolting leap of her heart was almost like a hammer-blow in her chest. His mouth touched hers lightly, captured her parted lips in his, began a series of small, teasing, devouring half-kisses which sent her temperature soaring dizzily.

'Dominick...' Her muffled plea escaped as he lifted his mouth for a moment to study her hot face.

'Yes?'

'Please, don't...' she gasped faintly. It was the opposite of what she wanted; it could only lead to heartbreak and misery, and she despised herself for it. She was quivering inside. He must be able to feel it. As if reading her thoughts, he gave a short laugh and dropped his mouth to silence her. The tantalising was over. The kiss deepened, escalated into a hungry urgency, blotting out the alarm bells in her head.

He tasted so good. Letting her body relax a fraction, she felt his hand snake down her back to press the arch of her waist. Taking a step closer, he brought their bodies into total contact, making her actively aware of the hard shape of his body. She shivered convulsively, and reached to cling to his neck. She couldn't help herself. Some perverse emotion shook her right down to the tips of her toes as his strength, his raw, uncompromising, arrogant maleness, enveloped her.

'I'm not sure getting to know you better is a wise course of action, Emma...' he murmured, finally releasing her. 'Because the more I get to know, the more I like...'

'The feeling is...mutual,' she heard herself confess huskily. It was nothing more than the truth, but a buried streak of common sense, of self-preservation, seemed to shrivel in despair at her gullible admission.

'Let's get out of this hellhole...' he grinned faintly, steering her towards the dangling rope ladder '...and get some air, shall we?'

She preceded him up the ladder. Never in her life before had she felt so conscious of the provocative swing of her hips, or of the way the tight jeans clung to the curve of her buttocks. Back in the second-floor tower room, she watched Dominick's dark head emerge from the trapdoor. Her throat felt dry as she forced a light smile.

'Come on,' he said coolly, taking her upper arm in a proprietorial clasp and steering her back downstairs. 'Messing about in boats is next on my agenda. I can show you some of the estate at the same time...'

The boat was moored in a tumble-down boathouse at the edge of the river, which bordered the Fleetwood land on one side. She'd somehow expected a flashy white motor launch. But the craft in question turned out to be a small, workmanlike narrowboat.

'It's ancient,' Dominick confirmed, with a casual grin. 'My father had a fixation about old canal boats. He bought this one for next to nothing from a boatyard that went out of business.'

Emma climbed on board, and walked slowly up and down the narrow side-ledges, past the faded narrowboat rose paintings in their peeling yellow and red and white, pushed open the swing doors at the far end. Inside, the fittings were amazingly good. The small kitchen had newish-looking pine units. Beyond, a pine table was flanked by green floral benches. Further in was a tiny bathroom with a perspex-fronted shower. There was a double bunk and two single bunks at the far end. She came back to inspect the kitchen cupboards curiously.

'There are cups, plates, glasses even! This is like a little floating doll's house! Can we take it out? Go for a cruise down the river?'

'I'll check on petrol. But I think we could make it down to a pub about half a mile away.' He smiled at her burst of enthusiasm. 'Anything to keep my new archivist happy in her job.'

'You're too kind,' she murmured, unable to suppress a laugh. Dominick gazed at her for a long moment, his amusement growing.

'You should laugh more often,' he advised wryly. 'It suits you.'

She tried to think of a neat, flippant retort, but failed lamentably. Instead, she blushed.

'So does blushing like a schoolgirl,' he teased, his eyes sliding over her with a darker gleam.

'Do you never stop poking fun at people?'

'Nope. It's my favourite technique in court. I poke fun at the judge.'

Catching her lower lip in her teeth, she suppressed a giggle.

'Let's get going,' she urged, a sudden surge of impatience taking over. 'I'm longing to float along the river in this gorgeous little boat...'

The slow, lazy pace of the narrowboat was extraordinarily relaxing. As they moved at a leisurely chug along the deserted river, Emma sat on the flat roof of the boat experiencing a sense of well-being almost piercing in its intensity. The April sun was hotter than she'd realised. All along the river banks, signs of spring were rampant. Pale green leaves, moorhens with fluffy little chicks. Through lacy overhanging trees the sky had turned a shade of china blue. She found herself noticing everything with sharp, brilliant clarity. A fizzy, effervescent sense of happiness was enveloping her. She hardly dared to question the reason for it because she knew it might burst and vanish, like a bubble floating in sunlight...

The pub was an up-market variety, an old beamed inn, with a well-tended garden fringed by weeping willows. The restaurant boasted an extensive wine list and cosy red candles. They tied the narrowboat to a handy post, and had an excellent lunch of home-made asparagus soup, followed by fresh salmon with new potatoes. They talked all the way through. Emma, with a moment's genuine surprise, couldn't think of anyone she'd met whose company she found so... compelling. By the time they'd finished the main course, they seemed to have discussed tastes in everything, from liking Provence, Picasso, the Tudor period in history and anything to do with

Greece, ancient or modern, to disliking Disney World, contemporary art and rave music.

'Could you manage any pudding?' Dominick gazed at her across the table, his eyes lazily humorous. 'There's chocolate cheesecake, which is pretty tempting...'

'How can I resist?'

'I'm hoping you can't,' he murmured, the rueful gleam in his eyes making her unsure whether the *double entendre* was intended to be as arrogant as it sounded.

They finished with coffee and liqueurs. Strolling down to the boat afterwards, through the families sitting outside with small children, she felt delightfully soporific. And dangerously happy...

'So what do you think of the boat?' She was sitting beside Dominick as he steered them back along the river.

'I love it. How come it's in such good condition inside?'

'Needs a little work,' he pointed out wryly. 'But this was my father's gesture at escapism...'

'Escapism?' She thought of Sir Robert Fleetwood, Dominick's father... A brief pang of her old bitter resentment returned, like an unexpected knife through her heart.

'He could chug off down the river on this, and no one would guess that they were looking at Sir Robert Fleetwood of Fleetwood Manor,' Dominick said expressionlessly. 'He could also forget that the house was rapidly deteriorating, and that he was married to my mother. He used this boat regularly, right up until he died . . .'

She was silent, absorbing this. Used the boat for *what*? she found herself wondering, her fists clenching. For a succession of secret trysts with women friends?

'Your father and mother didn't get on?' she said at last, picking her words carefully.

'They loathed each other,' he agreed ironically.

'What . . . what was the problem?' She hardly dared ask. The past, her knowledge of her mother's involvement, seemed to burn a hole in her brain.

'My father was a womaniser. He was always prone to philandering. But it got worse shortly after I was born.'

'Why . . . ?'

Dominick shot her a lidded glance. Had he noticed her acute tension? His tone was coolly amused as he went on, 'My mother didn't want any more children. I've a feeling they tossed a coin and my father lost the toss. He had the vasectomy, to save Mother having to be sterilised. The problem was that the vasectomy seemed to have an unfortunate effect on my father's masculine pride. He felt the need to seduce every passing female from then on to prove he was still a real man. My mother put up with it for so long, then an almighty row erupted. My father was locked out of her bedroom at night. As I recall they didn't even speak to each other for the next few years.'

'Poor you,' she breathed quietly. 'You . . . you must have felt the tension, as a child?'

'I was away at school most of the time. Being the younger son, I got off a lot lighter than Richard. If I bear any scars, they're not visible.'

'Are they ever?' Her cool query registered with him, and he gave her a hard glance.

'Sometimes they are,' he told her calmly, 'in the form of very visible chips on the shoulder, Emma.'

There was a silence. She found herself staring at him stupidly, her jaw sagging. Was he playing games with her, all the time? Knowing about her mother's involvement with his father?

'Loosen up,' he advised softly. He reached to brush his knuckles slowly along the smooth oval of her cheek. 'Whatever caused your scars, Emma, they fade when you relax. As you've been up till now.'

Speechless, she found herself locked in his gaze. Very carefully, he reached out and put a hand on her waist, and pulled her closer. His touch triggered wild reactions inside her. His warm fingers, through the white cotton of her shirt, seemed to scorch her.

This was insane, she reflected furiously. How could she react this way to Sir Robert's son, when in all probability Dominick's feckless father had seduced and begun an affair with her own mother, right here, in this narrowboat, over twenty years ago? A wave of fury overwhelmed her. She wrenched herself free of his hands, so abruptly that she almost fell over the side.

The narrow gaze had deepened. The gentian blue mirrored the blue of the sky and river in the warm April sun.

'Emma, you're quite safe,' he told her flatly. 'I'm not about to force you to do anything you don't want to do...'

Her emotions seemed to be on a kind of irrational see-saw, she reflected helplessly. The caution, the concern in his voice seemed to lift the abrupt curtain of misery. Just as fast as it had descended, it vanished again. The past receded. She was obsessed with the past. But the present was now, here, with this mounting pleasure in Dominick's company. The hazy bitterness, for something she didn't really know about, didn't really understand, seemed to drift back to an acceptably distant corner of her mind...

Then she stiffened in shocked alertness. The full impact of his words, the story he'd told her about his father, finally hit her.

Sir Robert had had a *vasectomy*? Shortly after Dominick was born? Dominick was ten years older than she was. Which meant that her father's anguished suspicions about Sir Robert being her true father were impossible. Her mother's affair with Sir Robert couldn't have led to conception of any kind...!

She realised that Dominick was watching her with narrowed, curious eyes which seemed to probe inside her head. Could he read her thoughts? Did he know how her brain was racing round in astonished circles of relief, and bewilderment...?

'Emma?' he prompted softly.

'Sorry,' she confessed in a small voice. 'I...I'm afraid that I over-react sometimes...'

'Did someone hurt you? Some man?' The husky voice held an edge of anger, and her heart seemed to contract with emotion.

'No. Nothing like that,' she hastened to re-assure him, turning determinedly away. Her heart was pounding like a drum against her ribs. Sir Robert had still caused her parents' marriage to break up. She still had every reason to feel bitter towards the Fleetwoods, to feel disloyal to her father for this crazy attraction towards Dominick...

He was guessing wrongly, suspecting that she'd had an unhappy love-affair, or some past sexual trauma... But did he actually *care*? About *her*? Her feelings were so muddled, she felt dizzy. But even so, with the ghastly, secret shadow of their brother-sister relationship dismissed, like a welcome bolt from the blue, it was easy, headily, seductively easy, just at this moment, to believe that he did...

CHAPTER FIVE

VANESSA BUCKINGHAM was sliding elegantly out of a white XR3 cabriolet as they walked back up from the river. The evening sun was slanting low on to the side of the manor, making the old bricks glow crimson, but Vanessa's appearance robbed the scene of any magic. Emma felt some of her hazy happiness vanish in a flash. The sense of threat was undefined, and she felt intensely confused, and annoyed with herself for feeling it at all...

'Dominick!' Vanessa had been heading for the entrance, then turned and caught sight of them out of the corner of her eye. She waved enthusiastically as she spotted their approach. But she ignored Emma completely as she ran to meet them, and kissed Dominick. Aiming for a politely bland expression, Emma watched the blonde girl slip her arm through his, and smile flirtatiously up at his dark face.

'I heard! On the grapevine!' she was exclaiming huskily. 'So sorry about poor Richard. But congratulations all the same! The new baronet! *Sir* Dominick Fleetwood, QC. It has a definite ring, don't you think?'

'If you say so.'

'Will you be going out there? To Tibet?'

'I don't know. I've several appointments in London on Monday,' Dominick murmured coolly. 'I'll make plans afterwards.'

There was a small silence as they all reached the front door.

'Are you coming in to join us for a drink?' Dominick made the suggestion casually. There was another pause while Vanessa glanced at Emma, her face a bright mask of sophistication. Was she calculating the exact meaning of 'us'? In tight cream jodhpurs and a cream silk blouse, and with the stunning bone-structure of an immaculately made-up face, the girl couldn't be feeling threatened, Emma felt sure. Vanessa Buckingham made her feel plain and dowdy and colourless.

'Love to, darling...' She hesitated, then added, 'Only I really came to discuss a legal matter— confidential, I'm afraid. Could I possibly have half an hour, Dominick?'

'Sure. Why not...?' He glanced down at Emma, his gaze blandly unreadable. 'Will you excuse us, Emma?'

'Of course. See you later...'

Before any more could be said, she escaped indoors, and bolted to her room. There, sitting on the faded grandeur of her bed, she grappled with the ridiculous turmoil of emotions seething inside her. She felt...how *did* she feel exactly?

The euphoria of discovering that she and Dominick weren't related was so intense, she couldn't remember ever feeling anything quite like it. It was a silly, floating, wildly relieved sensation. It was how she imagined she might feel on finding that some fatal disease had been wrongly diagnosed. That light, elated, champagne-filled sensation of escaping some imminent tragedy...

But it didn't make sense. Even without that shadow of uncertainty, she should distrust the Fleetwoods. She'd thought herself a relatively level-headed, logical person. But ever since she'd met Dominick, logic seemed to have died an abrupt death. How could she hate him, resent him for what he stood for, for the family he represented, and at the same time lap up the moments in his company with the pathetic eagerness of a devoted Labrador?

Standing up sharply, she marched to the mirror and glared at herself. Large grey eyes glared back beneath dark, well-defined eyebrows. Her eyes were probably her only redeeming feature, she reflected ruefully; they were a clear cloud-grey, dark-fringed and wide-spaced above the nondescript lines of a face too pale, too long, too wide-mouthed. The heavy chestnut hair was straggling down from its confines at her nape. A few strands hung down at her temples. All her make-up had disappeared, either because of the outdoors kind of day she'd just spent, or because Dominick had kissed her rather too thoroughly...

Be realistic, she told herself harshly. With Vanessa Buckingham as competition, Dominick could only be playing around, amusing himself

with his new archivist until the novelty wore off...
If she wanted to ensure that her emotions stayed
intact, she should keep that knowledge firmly in
her head...

She had a shower, washed her hair, and
swapped the denims and shirt for a calf-length
full skirt in blue and white cotton ticking, with
a soft blue scoop-necked T-shirt. Slipping slender
bare feet into flat leather sandals, she let her hair
hang loose down her back to dry, and found a
white cotton jacket in case the evening became
any cooler. She was making a fool of herself, she
told her reflection despairingly, if she let
Dominick see how much he disturbed her. Or else
she was being *made* a fool of, taken advantage
of, by a man with a 'social column' reputation
as a womaniser almost as infamous as his
father's...

The attics were the perfect retreat. She was engrossed in one of the letters to Sir George when
Dominick came in search of her. She stiffened as
she heard his step behind her.

'Quite a workaholic, aren't you?'

'I love my job.' She didn't glance up from her
work.

He was silent for a moment, as if assessing her
mood.

'Weekends are definitely for relaxing,' he reminded her calmly. 'I've come to see if you'll give
me a game of chess.'

'Chess?' She lifted her head and stared at him
in sudden astonishment. 'Look, you employed

me as an archivist, not as a handy partner for whatever leisure pursuit you fancy indulging in...'

He came over to prop himself nonchalantly on the edge of the desk. His gaze was veiled but amused. He was much too close. She had to use every scrap of self-control not to shift her chair a few inches further back. He'd changed his denim outfit for dark green cord trousers and a matching forest-green silk shirt. The colour seemed to darken his blue eyes to the shade of deep sea-water.

'Now what's triggered the frosty reception, I wonder?' he taunted softly. 'I thought we were getting along rather well earlier. What's wrong, Emma?'

'Nothing is wrong,' she explained, masking her nerves with a tone of extreme patience. 'Have you considered that maybe I'd prefer to decipher sixteenth-century papers than play chess with you?'

'Can my fragile ego stand such a blow?' The dark gleam in his eyes was too humorous for his words to be convincing.

'Besides, I'd have thought you'd be spending the evening with Vanessa...' The words were out, more sharply than she'd intended, too late to retract. The gleam grew more triumphant. Heat rushed to her face, and her heart began to thud dully in her chest.

'Vanessa?' Dominick's assumed look of blank incomprehension was masterly. 'Who is Vanessa?'

It was no good, she had to laugh. Shakily, she pushed her chair back, and faced him with a slightly uncertain gaze. He gazed back, his eyes suddenly serious.

'Emma, I had a brief chat with Vanessa,' he told her patiently. 'Then there was a lengthy phone call about the Fleetwood May Ball. I'd forgotten all about it.'

'May Ball? That sounds rather nice...'

'It's been hosted here as long as I can recall. But it's a charity thing—organised by the kind of ladies who love taking charge of things like that. I've said it can go ahead.' He gave her a searching look, and added casually, 'You can hire a ballgown and come, if you like...'

'Is it held in the Great Hall?'

'Yes.'

'Then how could I refuse?' She glowed at him, suddenly shy.

'Good. So how about chess?'

'I don't play very well...'

'That's OK. I don't have a problem with winning.' His slow grin turned her bones to water.

'No. I don't imagine you do.' She kept her voice level with difficulty, because the feel of his hand on her arm was shooting the now familiar, unsettling sparks of fire along her nerve-ends.

In the library, a fire was burning brightly in the black-oak fireplace. The flames licked hungrily round a log the size of a tree-trunk. In front of the fire, on a richly patterned square of red and gold Aubusson carpet, and flanked by a pair of velvet wing chairs, stood a low Sheraton card table. On the table was the most exquisite chess set she'd ever seen.

Emma gazed at it in awe. 'That is beautiful,' she breathed. 'How old is it?'

'Late eighteenth century. Probably.' Dominick went to sit on one of the chairs. He gestured briefly to her to sit opposite. She took her seat and faced Dominick's non-committal expression across the table separating them. There was a fluttering sensation in her solar plexus, and no amount of deep breathing would dislodge it.

'Is it Indian?' she ventured, gazing at the intricate delicacy of the carving.

'Cantonese. Carved in ivory, long before the world woke up to the iniquities of the ivory trade.'

As he spoke, he took two pieces, a black and a white, and switched them around behind his back, holding out his hands for her to choose.

'Your first move,' he confirmed wryly as she picked the white.

'I hate this.' She laughed, eyeing him warily. 'Facing a new opponent, having no idea what strategy they use...'

He watched with lidded eyes as she made her first move. Her fingers shook as she lifted the pawn and moved it two squares forward.

'Where did you learn to play?'

'My father taught me,' she said quietly, 'and I played a bit in the chess club at university. How about you?'

'I first learned at school. I've played on and off ever since...'

They were silent for a while as the familiar moves of the game progressed. The silence deepened. But, instead of the usual, intense concentration associated with previous games she'd experienced, this silence held layers of tension she'd never encountered before. The sonorous ticking of the clock on the chimney-piece, the soft hiss of the burning log sounded thunderously loud in this silence. Emma had never felt so self-conscious before, playing chess. Every time she reached a hand to select a piece, hovered to decide its direction, she felt as if Dominick's narrowed gaze singed her trembling fingers.

She had no idea how much time had passed before Mrs Shields delivered prawn and cream cheese canapés and a bottle of dry sherry. They were so engrossed, they hardly noticed her.

The housekeeper bustled about putting another log on the fire, drawing the heavy velvet curtains in the deep bay window to blot out the darkness. She hovered for a few moments, her eyes flicking curiously from Emma, curled in the chair, one foot hooked up beneath her, gazing intently at the chessboard as she wound a lock of hair round her forefinger, to Dominick, sprawled lazily in his chair, long legs stretched towards the fire.

Helpfully putting the canapés within reach of the games table, she poured sherry into the two crystal glasses.

'Will there be anything else, Mr Dominick?'

'Don't worry, Mrs Shields,' Dominick assured her smoothly. He hardly looked up from the board as he spoke. 'And thank you very much. If we need anything else, we can get it ourselves.'

When they were alone again, Dominick passed one of the sherry glasses across, and took a slow sip from his own. She met his eyes, conscious of the electrifying reaction whenever he looked at her that way...

The dark blue gaze moved lazily down, over her throat, over the generous curves hidden by the T-shirt. As she leaned forward to study the chessboard, the scooped neck of the powder-blue top revealed the valley between the firm globes of her breasts. She sat up quickly as she realised the view he must be studying. But changing position only seemed to make things worse. When she sat back, her nipples jutted, tell-tale hard and pointed, beneath the soft T-shirt fabric.

Dominick's face had darkened. As he shifted position lazily in his chair, crossing his long legs at the ankle, her eyes were pulled towards the strong bulge of muscle in his thighs. She felt a helpless surge of reaction. Her feelings were so mixed up, the melting warmth of suppressed desire was so strong, she was finding it more and more difficult to concentrate on the chess game.

She tried to take a grip on her feelings by thinking about Vanessa. Vanessa and Dominick obviously had a relationship of some sort. The way the blonde girl looked at him, the way she acted around him made that much abundantly clear. Emma got the impression that Dominick only had to click his fingers, and Vanessa would drop what she was doing and follow him to the ends of the earth if asked . . .

Wasn't that painfully close to the way she was feeling today? The parallel was alarming, but honesty forced her to confront it. Shivers of awareness shafted into her stomach, provoked a warm, aching sensation in her groin, and she closed her eyes and fought for control.

'Check,' Dominick murmured neutrally.

Her eyes shot open, just in time to see the lean brown fingers grasp a black knight, hop it neatly over her bishop to take her queen. She blinked, aghast at the speed with which he'd cornered her king.

'Not the shrewdest game I've seen.' Dominick grinned as she took a defensive counter-measure which would only delay her fate. 'But I suspect you've had other things on your mind tonight.'

She tensed. 'What makes you say that?' Her voice sounded husky, even to her own ears. If only he'd stop looking at her like that. As if he saw straight through her head, tapped into her thoughts.

'The look in your eyes,' he suggested softly, 'and the memory of how you responded to me last night.'

'Dominick . . .' Her throat had dried. She took a reckless gulp of sherry, and willed herself to stay calm.

'If I came to your bedroom again tonight,' he mused, hoarsely amused, 'would you respond with the same enchanting enthusiasm, I wonder?'

She stood up, bent on walking out, and he moved swiftly to block her path.

'Don't be a bad loser,' he murmured teasingly, hooking her round to haul her against him.

'I'm *not*——' Her angry retort was silenced by his mouth. And her noble intention of asserting herself vanished. He kissed her with that same tantalising rhythm, short, hungry snatches of passion which aroused her more headily than she could ever have imagined. In one of the brief respites, she gazed up at him blindly, her lips parted, her breathing shallow and restricted.

'God, I want you...' He shuddered as he pulled her down to the rug and pinned her there beneath him.

'Dominick...you can't...for God's sake, not *here*——' Her horrified protest was muffled by his mouth. And her brain switched off. The arrogance of his hunger, his assumption that she would consent, gave her a powerful surge of indignation. But her awareness of her own desire drowned out further protests before she'd even formed them. Being kissed by Dominick Fleetwood was like nothing she'd ever experienced before, a madness too strong to fight...

'You want me too,' he said on a thick groan. 'Admit it, Emma...'

'Yes,' she whispered faintly, 'I want you too...'

Writhing despairingly on the smooth weave of the antique carpet, with the warmth of the fire driving the temperature higher, she closed her eyes, shaking violently as he bent to deepen his kiss. When he pinned her there with his body, the captor with his prize, the reaction was explosive. The feel of his masculine weight aroused a primitive surge of surrender. And the release of knowing that her secret fear was groundless, that her feelings were not forbidden feelings, tipped the scales. Snaking her fingers into his hair, she returned his devouring kiss with a wantonness she didn't recognise, wouldn't have believed possible.

'You're beautiful...' The thickening in his voice was unbearably exciting. With an impatient, assertive gesture he pushed up her T-shirt, unfastened the clip of her white satin bra, and exposed her breasts to his view. Suddenly nothing on earth mattered except the need to feel that fierce swell of pleasure from his lips on her breasts. With a choked gasp, she reached up and caught his head, pulling him down to her. Mentally, she was a blank void. Physically, she was pliant and open, arching instinctively up to him, her feelings bewildering but overwhelming.

She shuddered with dizzy delight as his tongue teased each nipple.

'Do you like that?' The deep voice held a growl of sensual knowledge which was irresistible.

'Do I like it...? Dominick...this is... Oh, God, I don't know how to describe...' Her faint murmurs were swallowed back in her mouth as his lips bruised hers, his fingers cupping the rearing jut of her breasts, then raking hungrily down to the waistband of her skirt. He found the side-button, freed it, slid the cotton material down to her hipbones while he gazed wordlessly at the smooth curve of her stomach above the white satin triangle of her panties.

'Then don't try, sweetheart,' he growled unsteadily, 'because neither do I...'

Dropping his mouth to trail a line of tantalising kisses around the neat indent of her navel, and along the softness of her stomach, she tensed as he hooked a possessive finger inside the white briefs and eased them down.

'You're shaking,' he rasped softly. He was stroking the length of her body with long, sensual strokes which fanned the flames even higher. 'Don't be frightened of me, Emma...'

'I can't help it, but I want you... to make love to me...' The whisper was so faint, he didn't seem to hear. Abruptly, she was naked beneath his gaze, and her hands trembled even harder as she reached with the clumsiness of inexperience to help him off with his shirt, fumbled with the waist of his cord trousers.

'Hey, slow down,' he teased ruefully, catching her hands and sweeping them to his lips, before getting quickly to his feet. Shivering convulsively, she watched him cross to the door and turn the key. He was naked from the waist up, and she stared at him in the firelight. The light and shadow played over broad shoulders and tanned, lean-muscled torso. A sprinkle of dark hairs shaded the centre of his chest. The cord jeans fitted well over narrow hips. The shape of his sex was visible below the waistband, a rounded, powerfully male bulge which sent her pulses skittering crazily, and dried her throat with nerves...

'We wouldn't want to give my loyal old housekeeper a heart attack,' he murmured wryly, coming back to kneel beside her where she lay, curled now defensively on the rug, in the glow of the fire. He bent to kiss her again, with mounting hunger, easing her on to her back, sliding his hands along the silken inner plane of her thighs. 'I want to make this last as long as humanly possible, my beautiful little Emma...'

'Dominick, please...' What was she begging for? To her shame, she realised she was so aroused that she could feel the warm, welcoming moistness in the secret part of her that Dominick was lazily, unabashedly exploring with long, sensitive fingers. Heat enveloped her as his bold investigation grew more intimate, more demanding. Words died in her throat. The responses he was awakening were so piercing, so ferocious that she closed her eyes in astonished bewilderment.

'You have an incredible body,' he rasped softly, caressing the curves and hollows, the elongated line of upper arms and thighs, the full cushion of her buttocks, lingering again on the dark triangle of hair at the junction of her thighs until she bit her lip to keep from crying out.

'Dominick...'

'All right sweetheart, I'm all yours...' An air of potent urgency invaded the proceedings. Swiftly, with minimum effort, he dispensed with his own clothes. She was vaguely conscious of a brief pause while he extracted a discreet packet, donned a protective sheath. The thrust of his hard, hair-roughened thigh between hers seemed to focus every fibre of her being on the inevitability of what was happening. Too late now to have second thoughts, to use her powers of reason.

With a shudder, he prised her legs wide, captured the softness of her thighs, lifting her against him, probed with commendable gentleness against the taut, hidden entrance. The feeling was cataclysmic. Digging her nails blindly into his shoulders, she pulled his head down for the ecstasy and the reassurance of his kiss just as he lost control and drove, forcefully, right inside her.

The spark of pain felt like a burn, a tight, raw, tearing feeling. Her stifled scream was muffled against his mouth. But her tense resistance was all too noticeable. Dominick had stopped moving. He'd almost stopped breathing. Stunned, his gaze darkly incredulous, he lifted his head and stared into her set, white face.

'Stop,' she gasped idiotically. 'Please, stop it...'

'Emma...' The deep voice held layers of emotion, none of them decipherable. 'It's a little late to pull up the drawbridge, sweetheart.' The gleam in his eyes was definitely part humour, part anger. 'The defences are well and truly breached, my dear.'

'But I didn't . . .' She tossed her head from side to side in an agony of mortification, tears wetting her temples. 'I hadn't realised what it would be like . . .'

'And haven't still,' he soothed raggedly, humour replaced by that ruthless gleam of hunger. 'It's all right, Emma, trust me.'

'But . . .'

'Trust me.'

He'd begun to move again, slowly and deliberately, and to stroke her and touch her again with the utmost sensitivity, his lips on her forehead, her rumpled dark hair. A gradual change overcame her, erasing the discomfort, awakening all the surging hormones and blinding sensations that had led to this point.

'Better?' The wry whisper sent shafts of heat soaring through her bloodstream.

'Oh . . . *oh*!' The ripples in her stomach became an almost unbearable spasm, the physical reaction an almost spiritual one. Clenching every muscle in her body, she clung to Dominick in blind, explosive release, and with a choked murmur of laughter he crushed her to him and held her there, tightly moulded, branding her with his possession, until the unaccustomed ecstasy had finally subsided . . .

'What,' he said in a low, smiling voice, after an endless silence had enveloped them, 'would Mrs Shields say if she could see us now?'

'*Dominick* ...!'

'It's a fair conjecture,' he teased thickly, separating himself just a fraction to observe her pink cheeks with evident satisfaction. 'You were all for tearing off my clothes and having your wicked way with me, leaving the door unlocked. What a precipitate young lady you are, Emma Stuart.'

'Am I?' She gave a small, uncertain laugh. 'I hadn't realised I was until I met you...'

'Evidently. So what took you so long to experience the delights of sex?'

'Lack of... of the right person...?' It came out unbidden, and sounded horribly inane.

'Then my self-esteem knows no bounds,' he assured her gravely.

'Don't *mock* ...'

'Emma, I'm not mocking you.' He caught her chin as she began to twist her face away, and kissed her hard and long on her parted lips. 'I'm flattered. You don't know how it makes me feel, being the first, with a girl as desirable as you are.'

Happiness crept back, almost more powerful than the sensual experience of a few moments ago.

'Really?'

'Really. But why didn't you say something, Emma?'

'Like what?' She made a face. 'I didn't know quite how to put it. Besides, it went clean out of my head. Everything did. After last night, and today... all the time we've spent together... the chess game this evening...' She caught her breath on a shaky, nervous laugh. 'You seem to have an unfortunate effect on my brain-power!'

Dominick had reached for their clothes, and pulled on his trousers before handing her her skirt and top.

'I'm not being prudish.' His grin made her heart flip. 'I just don't trust myself not to repeat the entire procedure in a few minutes, if we lie here much longer.'

'Would that be . . . taboo?' Her genuine confusion made him laugh out loud, and pull her hard into his arms.

'You're adorable. No, it would not be taboo, my darling little Emma. But next time I'd rather make love to you in the comfort of a large bed.'

Next time? His calm assumption that there would be a next time made the blood course faster round her veins.

'What makes you so sure there'll be a next time?' she ventured, some of her normal spirit returning in the wake of the strength-sapping flood of desire.

'Because I want to marry you.' His deep voice held a teasing warmth and a hunger which turned her entire life upside-down in one short, heart-stopping moment. 'And while I imagine that a number of things could go wrong in being married to you, my sweet little Emma, I don't envisage a sexless future in single rooms . . .'

CHAPTER SIX

OVER the next few days, Emma began to understand how the princess must feel in the fairy-tales, swept off her feet by a handsome stranger, half afraid of him, secretly confused, but utterly besotted with him.

'Don't look so dazed,' Dominick teased her, whisking her up to London with him, ensconcing her in his Lincoln's Inn flat while he disappeared on high-powered court appearances, wining and dining her in sophisticated London style. 'This *is* going to work, Emma. Trust me, sweetheart...'

'You said you thought I was mixed up,' she ventured uncertainly, a flash of common sense and caution briefly making an appearance, 'and I must be! How come I've agreed to marry you, when a couple of weeks ago I told you I was wedded to my work and wanted to stay that way...?'

'No problem,' he observed with a lazy grin. 'This way you get me *and* your work—you can spend the rest of your days poring over old Fleetwood records. As long as you reserve your nights for me...'

He slid a proprietorial caress down to the V-fastening of her blouse, making her shiver with reaction. He was humouring her, she knew, hardly listening to her tentative objections.

'But everything is going so fast,' she breathed, when he kissed her with ruthless passion. 'How can you be so sure our marriage will work?'

'Wisdom and insight.' He grinned, his eyes smouldering with fresh desire. 'I see what I want and I go for it. Life's too short to weigh the pros and cons on every decision for twelve months.'

'Twelve months?' she echoed, with a shaky laugh. 'I'm lucky to be getting twelve *days* before you're whisking me off with your special licence!'

But her eyes were misty with happiness. If unwelcome, niggling doubts crept into her blithe infatuation, they only did so in the small hours of the morning. And with Dominick's warm male body beside her, one strong arm hooked across her ribcage, they dispersed again rapidly, like mist in morning sunshine, before they had time to take hold and shake her to her senses.

They were married in the thirteenth-century church in the grounds of Fleetwood Manor. Emma wore an ethereal, antique chiffon dress in faded clotted-cream shades. Her dark hair was wound up softly, and decorated with a wreath of lily of the valley. She carried a big bunch of stitchwort, Queen Anne's lace and bluebells, gathered from the grounds of the manor, and tied with a cream bow.

'You look like a sexy flower-fairy,' Dominick murmured, kissing her lightly as they signed the register afterwards. No fuss, the minimum of publicity, close friends and family only were Dominick's criteria. Lacking any family herself, she was happy to go along with it. A few couples who appeared to be very close friends of Dominick's were in church. And a cluster of her university friends came to wish them well, their eyes widening with envy as they assimilated where Emma and Dominick were going to live after the wedding.

Her friend Cathy, who was working a few miles away, had agreed in astonishment to be her bridesmaid. A petite girl with shiny red hair, she looked ravishingly pretty in a dress the colour of toasted almonds. Tobias, Dominick's best man, was a tall, rakish rugby player with a broken nose and laughing hazel eyes, who flirted outrageously with Cathy from the moment he saw her. But the entire event was a blur to Emma. She went through the motions, her head in the clouds, her feet barely touching the ground. Such had been her blinkered obsession with Dominick, she hadn't given a thought to his celebrity status. The appearance outside the church of journalists and photographers caught her by surprise.

Leaping from behind the massive old yew trees, the Press seemed to materialise out of nowhere. The barrage of clicks and flashes, the calls for quotes and interviews made her freeze in shock. Dominick's muttered curse won him a reproving glance from the vicar behind them. Tobias did an excellent job of fending them all off, and

Dominick and Emma escaped to the car, relatively unscathed.

'Looks as if we'll be all over the newspapers tomorrow.' Dominick's quick smile at Emma was half angry, half resigned. Jamie was at the wheel of the Rolls, heading back to the manor for the wedding breakfast proudly undertaken by Mrs Shields. 'My own bloody fault for trying to be secretive...'

'Why *were* you trying to be secretive?' She asked the question idly, her hand shakily in Dominick's, clasped on his hard thigh in his striped morning-dress trousers. She still felt dizzy, as if she was high on some non-existent drug. She was married to Dominick. She was Lady Fleetwood. Some great, mind-numbing whirlwind had swirled her up in its centre and spun her around so fast this last fortnight that she'd hardly been able to breathe, let alone think.

'Richard's death, mainly.' He glanced at her wryly. 'I know he died twelve months ago, but I've only just found out. I hadn't seen my brother for ten years. I can't feign a sense of deep bereavement I don't feel. But he was still my brother.'

'Yes. I see...'

'Decorum frowns on whirlwind marriages within ten days of hearing the news.'

'So...why the whirlwind?' she teased, her smile uncertain. Her cheeks were pink as she met his smouldering gaze.

'Because I was afraid you'd vanish into nowhere? Where you came from?' The murmur was huskily teasing.

'I didn't come from nowhere,' she reminded him, smiling. 'I was born here, remember?'

The blue gaze narrowed in amusement.

'So you were. The little gamekeeper's daughter. Welcome to your new home, Lady Fleetwood...'

They'd swept to a halt in front of the manor. Scooped from the car, helpless with laughter, she was whisked over the threshold of her future home, oblivious of the small group of guests arriving for the celebrations.

Her happiness was so intense, she was terrified. It couldn't last, said a nagging voice in her head. She'd jumped into this headlong, given herself no breathing space, ignored her reservations about the Fleetwoods, her bitter knowledge about her mother's fate.

But she loved Dominick. Of that she had no shred of doubt. And people *did* fall in love and marry in the space of a couple of weeks, didn't they? How could she have foreseen it? How could she have known that her apprehensive curiosity about her childhood home and its dark memories for her parents would lead her straight into the arms of the man she wanted to spend her life with?

She fiddled with her champagne glass in the shabby splendour of the manor's big diningroom, pretending to take part in the lively conversations going on around her, but her thoughts miles away. Cathy was chatting to her, her brown eyes alight with an excitement which struck Emma as having a lot to do with the proximity of Tobias. But she made absent replies, her brain tortuously picking over the story of her mother, her father's long-held bitterness about the Fleetwoods. She realised she was mentally justifying her impulsive behaviour...

'Emma?' Cathy's gentle prod brought her back to the present. 'Did you hear what I said?'

'Sorry? No.'

'When you rang and told me you were getting married, I did wonder if you were marrying the man or the house!' Cathy laughed, her eyes straying to Dominick's tall, dark frame a few feet away. 'But having met Dominick, all is revealed.'

'That doesn't say a lot for your opinion of my integrity,' Emma retorted wryly, 'if you thought me capable of marrying someone because they lived in an historic house!'

'Sorry——' Cathy's eyes twinkled with humour '—but I know how you used to talk about marriage. I'd privately decided that the only thing that would save you from spinsterhood was meeting someone with the means to keep a dedicated archivist happy!'

'That *is* a bonus.' Emma had to laugh, colour touching her cheeks at her friend's remark. 'But with Dominick it was——'

'Lust at first sight?' The deep drawl behind her made her spin round. Dominick bent to kiss her possessively on the mouth, long brown fingers caressing the delicate line of her throat at the scooped neckline of her dress. 'A mutual *coup de foudre*, Lady Fleetwood,' he added, on a husky murmur, softening the cynicism of his words.

Cathy gazed at them rapturously.

'This is *so* romantic!' She giggled. 'I shall never stop boasting. I'm a friend of *Lady Fleetwood*! Do you think I could use it to get discounts in local stores?'

'Definitely not.' Dominick grinned, straightening up. 'My father was notorious for not paying his bills. The Fleetwood name is probably mud around here.'

'Where are you two going for your honeymoon?' Tobias put in, coming to join them. He was a head shorter than Dominick, and stockier. But Emma could see what Cathy appeared to find attractive. Tough but kind, she decided.

'It's a secret,' she told Tobias, making a face. 'Dominick won't tell me.'

'But you'll love it,' her husband assured her softly, his blue gaze warming on her pretended annoyance. 'Trust me...'

'Trust me'. How many times had he said that to her? she reflected, meeting his eyes and feeling that familiar stir of desire.

'He's just worried I'll organise a strip-o-gram gorilla for your first night,' Tobias quipped, slapping Dominick on the back. 'Aren't you, Dom?'

'I wouldn't trust you as far as I could throw you,' Dominick agreed calmly. 'Now get lost, Tobias, I want to take my wife to bed.'

'*Dominick*...!' Outraged, but half melting with reaction, she found herself hauled out of the dining-room and practically frog-marched upstairs. 'Dominick, I hope this caveman act isn't typical,' she managed breathlessly, when he shut his bedroom door and shot her a smouldering grin. 'Maybe I should have spent a little longer getting to know you properly?'

'I warned you I was no gentleman,' he purred teasingly, his eyes slits of glittery blue between narrowed dark lashes. 'So take your bridal clothes off, my sweet Lady Fleetwood. I want to inspect the goods.'

'Why, you...!' Her flare of indignation made her run at him and thump her fists on his chest, but the anger was so wrapped up in laughter and desire, it fizzled out into mounting passion which consumed them both in its fire.

Afterwards, naked and entwined on the bed, their formal wedding clothes scattered disrespectfully to the four corners of the room, Emma gazed at Dominick with wide, thoughtful grey eyes.

'Calling it "Lust at first sight"... You didn't only marry me for sex, did you?' She laughed shakily.

'Naturally.' He hauled her over to lie on top of him, and she shivered with fresh desire. 'Sex, and general drudgery, of course. I thought I'd sack Mrs Shields and get you to do all the housework and cooking. Is that OK?'

'Whatever my lord and master desires,' she teased huskily. Sobering, she stared down into his blue eyes. They were an unfathomable quantity, she realised, with a sudden jolt of fear. His gaze was blandly unreadable.

'But . . . seriously——' her throat was suddenly dry '—you do . . . you do love me?'

He gazed back for a long, expressionless moment. Cupping her hot face in his hands, he examined her with wry intent.

'What do you think?'

The coolly ambiguous response made her heart contract. Her whispered questions had sounded ridiculously ill-timed, even to her. She should have thought of this before, a prosaic voice nagged in her head. She shouldn't need to ask her new husband such a question on their wedding-day! Marry in haste, repent at leisure? Was that what her parents would have said . . . ?

'Dominick . . .'

'What an insecure soul you are,' he silenced her, rolling her beneath him and dropping a hard, devouring kiss on her trembling mouth. 'Sweet little Emma, trust me. Everything——' He kissed her again, with a touch more gentleness. 'Everything is going to be all right . . .'

The newspapers had a field-day, but she and Dominick left for the secret destination that evening, which turned out to be a fast, no-queues private jet to Athens, and a magnificent suite in the city's oldest and grandest hotel on Syntagma Square.

'I thought we might be going to Paris in the spring,' she breathed, laughing with excitement and happiness. They were strolling through the narrow, sun-warmed streets of the Plaka, the old part of the city below the Acropolis. 'But Athens is just about my favourite place in the whole world!'

'Even though it's so crowded with tourists?'

'I know it's a bit touristy in places, but I love it. I spent a couple of summers in Greece. And the people have *soul*. They're...passionate. They like people to be in love!'

'They say Paris is the city of lovers, but I think Athens is better,' Dominick confirmed solemnly. 'It's warmer. More conducive to long, sensual nights...'

'Mmm...' She shot him a sideways look which was half shy, half dreamily aroused. They'd arrived late evening yesterday, and they'd made love all night. Her initiation into the complexities of sexual desire had flowed swiftly on from that first rapturous experience into layer upon layer of need and emotion, uncharted depths which had her reeling with shocked pleasure. A simple exchange of glances brought a subtle meltdown of desire which contracted her stomach, dissolved her thighs to jelly...

'It had to be Greece,' he agreed, smiling down at her flushed cheeks with a glint of teasing in his eyes. 'When you told me you were a classics graduate, and how you're crazy about Greek bouzouki music, I knew that only the cradle of civilisation would do...'

'How can you mock,' she demanded reprovingly, 'when we're behaving in such a madly romantic fashion?'

'Maybe I'm insecure?' He grinned, but there was a faint shadow in his eyes she didn't understand.

'*You*?' she teased. 'Insecure?'

They'd stopped at a well-known taverna in the Plaka for a typically Greek late lunch. A mouth-watering aroma of roast lamb filled the air. A richly flavoured wine from the barrel made her senses swim.

'Maybe you only married me for... security?' he suggested, shrugging lazily. 'Your father died recently. Maybe I'm a substitute father-figure?'

'You're only ten years older than me,' she pointed out lightly, 'so that's not very likely.'

'Maybe you only married me for my money?'

'Dominick...!' She stared at him, trying to fathom his mood. Dark and broodingly mocking, he looked so devastatingly attractive sitting across the red-checked table that she felt her heart begin to thud faster. He was casually dressed in loose navy shirt, fawn pleat-front trousers. His shirt-sleeves were pushed to his elbows, showing the tanned strength of his forearms. The lean brown fingers drummed faintly on the table as she watched him.

'Or maybe you only married me to get to be Lady Fleetwood?' His mouth quirked wryly as he saw her mounting anger.

'I married you...' She stopped, drawing a deep breath to control her voice. 'I married you because I fell in love with you,' she whispered, half laughing, half furious, 'and... and I wanted to be with you...'

Their eyes locked for an endless time. His gaze was veiled, smokily lidded, a deep ocean-blue she could drown in. She felt aware of his appraisal on every inch of her body. Her short, loose V-necked floral dress and flat, strappy brown sandals felt invisible, or transparent. For a few seconds she felt as if she was sitting in front of him, naked and vulnerable, in the crowded, noisy restaurant.

'Emma...' His wide mouth twitched slightly. He reached across the table, took her left hand. Turning her knuckles slowly towards him, he inspected the new rings on her slender finger. The engagement ring they had chosen together in London, antique gold set with a vast solitaire diamond. The wedding-band, wide and traditional and worn to a soft dull gleam over the years, had belonged to his great-grandmother. She'd accepted it with joy faintly tinged with fear. She hoped his great-grandmother's marriage had been happier than his parents'...

'Emma, I was teasing...' The husky humour in his voice dispelled some of her anger. 'Don't take everything I say so seriously, sweetheart.'

'So when you keep saying, "Trust me,"' she managed unsteadily, 'I shouldn't take you seriously?'

'I'll let you be the judge of that,' he murmured, lifting her hand and kissing the back of her fingers with a lingering sensuality which sent the brief moment of discord evaporating into the cheerful atmosphere of the restaurant around them. 'You are my wife, Emma. Always remember that. I will never do anything to hurt you...'

The rest of the meal was a blur. The only urgent goal was a mutual need to finish, walk back to the hotel...

'Let's take a bath,' Dominick drawled huskily when they'd regained the privacy of their room, pulling her into the outrageously luxurious bathroom and flicking on the gold taps of the huge sunken marble bath.

'A cool one?' she breathed, with a shudder of anticipation. She was abruptly transported to that rich dark world of sensuality he could trigger with a mere click of his fingers. Trembling with helpless excitement, she felt his hands grasp her shoulders, twist her round, seek the zip at the back of her dress. Sliding it purposefully down, he turned her again to survey the feminine curves, the taut hollows of her body. Her skin felt slightly damp with perspiration in the languid heat of the afternoon. A trickle of sweat ran down between her breasts. She felt her stomach heat, tighten with desire...

'Nothing could cool me down...' he said hoarsely. He was flinging off his clothes with careless impatience, revealing the powerful arousal of his body. He unfastened the slip of cream bra to expose her full breasts to his gaze. Her nipples were already stiff as he brushed his hands across the sensitive tips, then dropped his mouth to suckle each one as he pushed her lacy briefs down her trembling thighs. 'I'm so hot for you, I'm in flames, my darling...'

'Oh, Dominick!'

As he lifted her at the waist, she wound her arms round his neck while he wrapped her legs around him, smoothing her thighs closer with devastating sensuality, and stepped down into the bath. The water was scented with sandalwood essence. It felt silky, lukewarm on her skin. She found herself captured, sitting face to face, clinging to his muscular shoulders, strong masculine arms locked round her back.

The deep blue gaze was devastatingly sensual, heavy lidded, lazily darkened with carnal knowledge. Her breasts were pressed to the coarse plane of his chest, her thighs spread wide around the hard male hips. With the probing demand of his shaft positioned at the secret juncture where she was melting, heating, aching with need, it was the most erotic moment she could ever remember. With an agonised gasp of desire, she felt him propel her upwards to tease her taut nipples with his teeth, and then force her fiercely down, impaling her with ferocious hunger, kissing

her soft moans of ecstasy back into her throat.
The excitement and shivery, feverish rapture went
on, and on, and on...until the rest of the hot,
languorous afternoon stretched magically ahead
in the private bliss of their own making...

Fleetwood Manor, with its tranquil old walls and
peaceful backdrop of gardens, was quite a contrast when she stepped out of the car on to the
crunch of the drive a week later. The chill of the
English spring came as a shock to the system.
Emma shivered, even in her smart new suede
jacket and wonderfully cut gaberdine trousers
which Dominick had insisted on buying her from
one of the pricey boutiques in Athens. They'd
come home via London. Dominick had been
adamant that he should take her to Harrods, to
buy her a gown for the May Ball. It was in a big
box in the back of the car, its silky silver-grey
simplicity carefully packed in layers of tissue
paper...

'You look glowing, Lady Fleetwood,' Mrs
Shields informed her, smiling, as they went into
the hall. Dominick caught Emma's flush of
awkward embarrassment, hearing the title used
by the housekeeper, and angled a sardonic glance
at her when they were upstairs in the bedroom.

'You're going to have to come to terms with
your new title sooner or later,' he pointed out
calmly, coming to stand behind her as she sat at
the dressing-table brushing her long chestnut
swath of hair, 'like it or not.'

'It's going to take some getting used to.' She glanced up as he bent to stroke her neck and shoulders, bent his head to drop a kiss in the sensitive hollow behind her ear. 'Don't forget I'm only the *gamekeeper's* daughter!'

'Don't start that nonsense again, sweetheart.'

'But it's true. My father was on the same...the same *social* level as Mrs Shields!'

'To hell with social levels. You're my wife. That, my sweet little Emma, puts us on the same level. *Comprends*?'

'Yes...'

'I'm due in court tomorrow,' he reminded her, his fingers seeking the swell of her breasts beneath the gold silk of her blouse, making her catch her breath helplessly as he found the jut of her nipples and ruthlessly squeezed them into arousal. 'I may have to spend a couple of nights in London. Are you sure you want to stay here and work in those draughty old attics?'

'No. But I'll be just as lonely in your flat, while you're strutting about in your QC's wig...'

'I shouldn't give in to you,' he murmured throatily. 'I should drag you with me by the hair...'

'You promised me your caveman behaviour was just an act.' She laughed, shuddering with mounting need, twisting round as he ripped open the last button on her blouse, and exposed the ripe fullness of her breasts for his delectation.

'I thought it was.' He picked her up and carried her purposefully to the bed, proceeding to remove the remainder of her clothes and pin her there with the triumph of an outlaw. 'Now I'm not so sure. Maybe marriage is bringing out more Stone Age qualities in me than I realised...'

'I can vouch for that...' she said breathlessly as the inevitable passion overtook them. She shuddered in urgent surrender beneath his tender onslaught. 'I must have a secret fetish for Neanderthal man...'

'Show me...' he murmured thickly, teasing her ear with his tongue until the sensations made her squirm with delight. 'Show me this secret fetish of yours, Lady Fleetwood...'

She felt so hot, she could be back in Athens, in the lush warmth of the Greek climate. 'I want you...I love you and I want you...so much.' She caressed and explored him with rising audacity, seeking the powerful shaft of his manhood, stroking the glorious strength of him with slim, trembling fingers until he gave a hoarse moan and caught her small hand tightly in his.

'Careful.' He laughed softly. 'I want it to last, sweetheart...in fact, every time I make love to you I want it to last longer and longer...'

Rolling her on to her stomach, he straddled her, slid his hands beneath her ribs to cup the heavy fullness of her breasts. With bold arrogance, he parted her thighs and probed the delicate moistness with a sureness that sent fierce agonies of desire stabbing through her so powerfully that she convulsed almost instantly when he thrust inside her, her spasms of release making him shout his own victorious pleasure to the four walls of the bedroom...

He was away for three nights. It felt like three years. He rang her whenever he had ten minutes' break in court, and he rang her from his flat at night, when she was in bed, murmuring wickedly audacious things to her that made her glow from head to toe with rekindled desire.

On the day he was due back, Emma sat alone in bed, and took stock of all the upheavals of the last few weeks.

There was a wickedly indulgent tray of breakfast and morning papers on the table beside her. This had become a regular morning habit since Dominick had gone to London, partly because Mrs Shields insisted, and partly because with all the sudden, hectic excitement of the wedding, the honeymoon, and becoming the lady of the manor, she was feeling decidedly nauseous and shaky when she woke up in the mornings.

How, she wondered faintly, had all this heady, romantic adventure happened to her? She'd come here, nervous and cautious, unsure of her feelings about the job, the place, the family, the past... and here she sat, just over a month later, Lady Fleetwood, eating breakfast in bed, wife of the new owner of this magnificent manor house, with all its lands and its contents... The knowledge made her head reel, and somehow made her feel a deep, stabbing sense of guilt and unease.

The source of the unease became slowly apparent as she searched her heart. She hadn't been entirely honest with Dominick. She hadn't told him about the sordid little liaison between her mother and Dominick's father, Sir Robert. She'd never mentioned how she'd been nursing vague feelings of resentment towards his family, when she first came here...

More unsettling still, she hadn't told him about her secret fears that he could have been her half-brother...

She took a cautious sip of the freshly squeezed orange juice and eyed the golden texture of the toasted roll with faint queasiness. She'd woven her own tangled web of deceit, without meaning to. As soon as Dominick came back, she'd tell him. Bring the whole sorry affair into the open. Then maybe she'd stop feeling this sense of impending doom, hanging over her head like that mythical Greek sword, waiting to chop down her happiness just when she couldn't imagine ever feeling happier...

The housekeeper tapped at the door, and announced that a visitor was waiting for her in the library.

Emma's heart thumped nervously. Somehow, the reality of being Lady Fleetwood was only just sinking in. A visitor? Some cantankerous aristocratic relative of Dominick's, furious at the rapid secrecy of his marriage? She pictured some thin, coldly disapproving aunt, eyeing her up and down through a lorgnette. When Mrs Shields told her it was only Vanessa Buckingham, she felt a wave of relief.

'Tell her I'll be down in ten minutes.'

As she quickly pulled on jeans and white sweatshirt, and bundled her brushed hair into a ponytail, she tried to formulate a diplomatic greeting. Dominick hadn't invited Vanessa to the wedding. Was she here with congratulations? Or had she come to tell Emma precisely what she thought of her?

Hiding her trepidation, Emma breezed into the library, and gave Vanessa her warmest smile.

'How lovely—my first visitor!' she laughed. 'Can you stay for coffee?'

In short black skirt, city court shoes and black and white checked jacket, Vanessa Buckingham looked as poised and well-groomed as Emma felt casual and dishevelled. She was standing at the long casement windows, which looked out over a sloping lawn towards the distant bluebell woods. Turning round, she smiled at Emma with visible lack of warmth.

'No. I don't think so. This is just a flying visit to see how Dominick's new bride is coping with married life.'

Vanessa's voice was pleasant, but her tone was brittle. There was an underlying mockery. Emma kept her own smile glued in place.

'Ecstatically, thanks,' she managed lightly. Vanessa was definitely not one of life's good losers, she reflected wryly. 'Sorry about the wedding service—Dominick wanted us to marry quickly and quietly. It was just very close friends and family really...'

Vanessa laughed.

'God, what a naïve little fool you sound!' she said softly. 'Do you think I didn't know about the wedding?'

'I'm afraid I don't follow...' She stared at the blonde girl in mounting confusion, and Vanessa's eyes narrowed to incredulous slits of green.

'Good grief, he really hasn't told you, has he? Don't tell me he's pretended to fall in love with you, and you've believed him?'

'I think you'd better go!'

'Obviously the little gamekeeper's daughter was even more gullible than he imagined!'

There was a heavy sickness in Emma's stomach. Woodenly, she said, 'I haven't any idea what you're talking about...'

'I'm talking about the inheritance, darling. The conditions imposed by Sir Robert. Richard dropped out with his monks in Tibet, so Sir Robert specified that when he inherited he must marry within two months to qualify for the house and land. So Dominick was stuck with the same stupid conditions...'

'Are you trying to tell me——' Emma tried to sound coolly unconcerned, but her voice came out in a whisper '—that Dominick only married me to comply with some... some conditions in his father's will?'

'Goodness me, the penny's dropped,' Vanessa agreed silkily. 'My problem being that I'm

married, separated and still waiting for a divorce,
dear *Lady* Fleetwood. Another little problem was
that old bastard Sir Robert's other condition—
that his heir needed to produce a child within a
year of marriage to inherit Fleetwood Manor...
Unfortunately, I can't have children. So you're
the lucky female to beget the Fleetwood heir...
What did you think Dominick and I were dis-
cussing so urgently the other day in his study?'

Vanessa's words felt like physical missiles, her
triumphant, red-painted mouth very prominent
in the pale beauty of her face.

'I don't believe you...'

'But you actually believed a man like Dominick
Fleetwood could be madly in love with a little
nonentity like you? In the space of...what? Three
weeks? You may be satisfactory in bed, dear, but
a man of Dominick's standing would ideally
choose a lot more than *that* as a reason to marry!'

Was it true? The love she thought they shared
was so new, the marriage so hastily arranged...
Abruptly, with unbearable accuracy, she recalled
Dominick's probing questions about her marital
status, at her interview, recalled his mention of
eccentric conditions in his father's will... Everything Vanessa said was plausible, and horribly
possible...

The sick feeling grew stronger. It grew violently stronger. She felt as if she was falling,
silently into some aching void. The library blurred
and swayed. Emma had a strong stab of panic

that she was going to faint. She clutched at the edge of the sideboard near her, and missed. Then the polished boards dissolved into a black hole at her feet ...

CHAPTER SEVEN

'DO YOU feel all right now?' Jamie came awkwardly to find her where she sat on a secluded bench behind the high hedges of the Elizabethan knot-garden. His fresh complexion was pink with concern. 'Gran sent me to check on you.'

'Yes, fine. I just needed some fresh air...' She directed a determinedly bright smile at him as he came to sit beside her. She'd only been unconscious for a few seconds. Vanessa had summoned Mrs Shields. A glass of water had been fetched. Expressing false concern and wishes for her full recovery, Vanessa had roared away in her XR3. There was a peacefulness about the knot-garden that Emma loved. She'd escaped out here, found the sun-warmed bench, and managed to stave off conscious thought so far simply by gazing blankly at the intricately cut box hedging forming the twisted, flower-filled knot shapes in the flower beds.

'Lady Fleetwood...'

'Don't call me that!' The words came out with such fierce aversion that he blushed, his eyes clouding with fresh embarrassment.

'Emma, then,' Jamie substituted unhappily. 'I...I overheard what Miss Buckingham said...'

126

She turned slowly to look at him. 'Eavesdropping?'

'I couldn't help it. I was weeding under the library window. She was standing right by it. I heard every word.'

Emma felt the emotion rise up in her throat, and she swallowed hard.

'Did...did you believe it?' she whispered shakily.

Jamie shrugged slightly. He was about her own age, with an open, likeable face and a thatch of untidy brown hair.

'I'm not sure. But I really like you, Emma. I don't like seeing you hurt...'

'Oh, Jamie...!' She burst into tears. It was an idiotic thing to do. Self-pitying, pathetic, she knew. But she felt self-pitying and pathetic. These last few days, she'd been feeling gloriously happy but strangely vulnerable, shaky and tender inside, prone to extremes of emotion she'd never known before. Now, with Vanessa's words drilling themselves into her brain, suspicion and fear in her heart, she felt as if her whole life had abruptly disintegrated into nightmare...

The tears flowed, and she couldn't stop them. She found herself sobbing blindly against the grubby front of his gardening shirt. Jamie put a shaky arm round her and patted her back clumsily, as if she were an animal needing reassurance.

The crunch of the footsteps on the gravel path came too late to act as a warning.

'Well, well . . .' Dominick's voice cut across the scene with sardonic humour. She sprang away from Jamie, and Jamie jumped to his feet, such eloquent guilt in every line of the young man's body that Dominick's mouth twitched with suppressed laughter. 'This looks cosy. Can my new wife have been driven to seek consolation with my gardener after only three nights alone?'

'Sir, it wasn't——'

'That's all right, Jamie,' Dominick cut in with ominous calm. 'Get back to work, will you?'

Jamie shot a last worried glance at Emma's tear-drenched face, and turned and marched stiffly away. Dominick watched him go, then turned to her with that mocking tilt to his eyebrows that she knew only too well.

'What's going on, Emma?' Impeccable in his dark grey suit and ice-white shirt, he stepped closer and reached to grasp her shoulders. His mood was hard to fathom. Through the sting of tears, she had the vague impression that he was more amused than darkly jealous. Presumably Dominick had far too high an opinion of himself to imagine that his new wife would involve herself with the gardener-handyman. Far too much confidence in his wife's blind adoration to suspect her of such behaviour. . .

'Do I get an explanation? Or do I have to put two and two together and come up with some wildly improbable conclusion?'

'Vanessa came to see me this morning,' she managed in a muffled voice. His touch on her shoulders sent furious tingles down her arms. With a supreme effort, she pulled herself together, and managed to shake herself free of Dominick's grasp.

'Vanessa? Did she upset you?' The deep voice held a harder note.

'You could say that…' Drawing a deep breath, Emma faced him as calmly as she could. Silently he dug in his breast pocket and handed her a laundered white handkerchief. His dark face was suddenly devoid of expression. The blue gaze was bleakly intent. She took the handkerchief and scrubbed her wet face, balling it in her fist, unsure how to continue, how she dared say the words she had to say.

'Emma, tell me why you were crying.'

'She told me why you married me!' she whispered hoarsely.

There was a thunderous silence. She could hear her own heartbeat, mechanically fierce against her breastbone. Dominick didn't move a muscle.

'Really?' He spoke flatly, no trace of emotion. But his eyes were watchful, slightly narrowed. 'And why was that?'

'To inherit Fleetwood Manor. Because of the condition attached to the inheritance,' she persisted huskily. 'The…the one that stipulated that Richard must marry within two months of Sir Robert's death.'

Dominick's face was blank, his eyes unreadable.

'I see. So... let me get this straight. I'm supposed to have deliberately seduced you? Tricked you into marrying me? To comply with my father's will?'

She stared at him. Her heart was pounding. Her stomach was clenched into a tight, sick ball. But Vanessa's words echoed in her head. It made such ghastly sense. The speed, the secrecy of the marriage, the sheer unlikelihood of someone like Dominick falling in love with a little nobody like her...

'Yes...'

'And you believe this?'

This was like conversing with an automaton, she thought wildly.

'You... you told me there were eccentric conditions Richard had to comply with... when you talked about tracing him...' she said in a choked, tight voice.

'So I did.' Dominick's expression had hardened. 'So the evidence is stacked against me, is it, my trusting little bride?'

'You're obviously not going to deny it,' she said, her voice low and shuddery with emotion, 'because you can't! You might at least have had the good manners to tell me. But then I suppose *I* should have come clean about my reasons for marrying you!' She drew a deep breath, giving a sarcastic edge to her voice. 'Maybe this makes us quits? Checkmate, really?'

Appalled at her blurted defence, she swung away quickly, but not fast enough. The lean hand fastened with implacable strength on her shoulder, and spun her round again.

'Emma, what in the name of black hell are you bleating about?'

'You don't know, do you?' she spat furiously. She hardly knew what she was saying. It was as if all her bittersweet confusion of the last few weeks was rising up, like an invisible army, inside her. 'How your father *ruined* my parents' lives? *Seducing* his gamekeeper's wife, sacking them both when the affair became known... Remember you said you thought I was hiding something? That I was secretive? For a while I...I thought we could be brother and *sister*...!'

Slowly, a stunned look crossing his face, Dominick let his hand slide from her shoulder. He was staring at her as if she were a stranger. She felt like one. Abruptly, she felt as if she was flinging furious insults at a man she didn't know at all...

'And...were we?' The clipped fury in his voice made the tiny hairs at her nape prickle with fear, and anger.

'No! Do you think I'd have *married* you if we were?'

'Right now I find I'm not sure what to think. This seems to be a day for surprises.' The cutting edge of sarcasm was so cruelly icy, it flayed her in spite of her own fury.

'*Surprises*? Well...well, believe me, by the time our sham marriage is over, you're going to wish you'd never got involved with Jack and Amy Stuart's daughter!'

'At least I know now what you were hiding,' he said finally. His expression was unfathomable. 'When, precisely, did you satisfy yourself that our relationship wasn't potentially... *incestuous*?'

Colour flamed in her face. His scathing tone made him sound like a cynical prosecuting counsel.

'That day on the narrowboat. When... when you said Sir Robert had a vasectomy. I... I knew then...'

'How convenient of me to mention it...' he drawled.

'Oh, there you are, Sir Dominick!' The housekeeper appeared round the hedge, her face a triumph of diplomatic restraint. 'The doctor's here, Lady Fleetwood. He's waiting for you in the library.'

'The *doctor*?' Dominick's tone was ominously neutral, but there was a sharper gleam in his eyes.

'I fainted,' Emma told him shortly, 'but there really wasn't any need for the doctor——'

'On the contrary,' Dominick cut in decisively, slipping a firm arm round her shoulders and steering her ruthlessly towards the house. 'If my *wife* faints, I want to know why.'

Emma felt as if she'd jumped on a rollercoaster ride which was veering dangerously out of control. The nightmare element to the day was intensifying.

The doctor was middle-aged and kindly, with a weather-beaten face and a tweed jacket which looked as if he'd worn it non-stop all his life. In the privacy of the bedroom, he examined Emma thoroughly, and gave her a wry smile as he clicked his black bag shut and straightened up.

'Plenty of iron. You're a bit anaemic. I'll prescribe you some tablets. Otherwise, you should have a fairly trouble-free pregnancy, Lady Fleetwood.'

'*What*?' The faint jerk of reaction drew a surprised look.

'Didn't you suspect? Morning sickness, dizzy spells?'

'No. I... No, I didn't...' This *was* a nightmare, she decided miserably. Soon she'd wake up, breathe a sigh of relief, and the day would start over again normally, happily, full of excitement and secret bliss and shivers of anticipation...

When the doctor left her, and she lay there assimilating this latest development, the ghastly truth filtered in, finally and convincingly. Vanessa's poisonous words were true. No wonder Dominick had scarcely left her alone since their wedding-day. No wonder he made wild, passionate, unprotected love to her at every possible opportunity...the urgency was explained now, with a sickening clarity. Less to do with untrammeled desire, more to do with the need to get his new wife pregnant as fast as possible, fulfil the last condition attached to the will...

She stared at the engagement and wedding rings on her hand. Her eyes blurred with tears. Diamonds were forever? The sparkle of the precious diamond refracted into a thousand tiny pin-points of light in her distorted vision. She couldn't recall ever feeling so utterly wiped out. So betrayed...

And yet... a stubborn, stupid little core of joy and pride asserted itself, in spite of the disaster of her marriage. She was going to have a baby? A new little life was growing inside her, already? Dominick's baby...

Too late, reality crashed back. She'd forgotten to beg the doctor not to tell Dominick. In her shocked astonishment, she'd let him walk out, go back downstairs, and presumably at this very moment he'd be advising the proud father on his wife's need for plenty of rest and iron pills...

'Emma?' Dominick came into the bedroom, pushing the door shut behind him with a decisive click, the expression on his face too coldly arrogant to signify ignorance. 'Paul's just told me... Congratulations, my darling Lady Fleetwood. I didn't expect to be provided with an heir quite so quickly.'

His voice was laced with sarcasm. She winced, sitting up quickly and facing him with a deep tremor of apprehension. Suddenly she'd never felt so vulnerable, so open to physical or emotional attack, in her entire life...

'Please... go away...'

'That's no way to speak to your husband, and the father of your child, Emma.'

'Dominick——'

'And whatever twisted little schemes are going on in your beautiful head, believe me I'm a firm believer in the sanctity of marriage,' he continued, his drawl provocatively cool and insulting, 'and in the need for a healthy sex life between married couples...'

'If you touch me, I'll——'

'You'll what?' Coming to sit on the edge of her bed, he slid a hard palm round to her nape and tilted her chin up with his thumb. 'Scream? Snatch up a weapon and attack me? You know, it's going to take some time to come to terms with this abrupt change in our relationship, Emma, darling. I still find it rather hard to believe that I left a loving, pliant partner three days ago, and have returned to a vengeful little wife from hell.'

'You can't deny those conditions Vanessa told me about, can you?'

'It seems to me there's very little point,' he agreed cuttingly. The dark gleam in his eyes was making her tremble, right to the very centre of her soul. 'I've been tried, found guilty and sentenced in my absence. And all along, if I'm to believe it, my new wife has been plotting some dramatic revenge for the sins of my father.'

She stared at him mutely. He made her wildly impulsive declaration of self-defence sound utterly absurd. Which, she had to admit, it was. But his cool conceit was intolerable.

'Why did you do it, Dominick?' she whispered.
'Do what?'

'Use me. Pretend to fall in love with me, sweep me along on this farcical whirlwind marriage of yours, when all along it was because you were up against a . . . a legal deadline. Even down to *having* to get me pregnant. To provide an heir within a year of marriage. What a push-over I've proved to be, haven't I? Even in *that* respect!'

The last accusation hung in the air like an unexploded bomb. He expelled his breath slowly. The gleam in his eyes had grown darker. Heavy-lidded, trained intently on her white face, his eyes were suddenly smoulderingly, terrifyingly furious.

'So,' he drawled icily, 'I married you to inherit the manor, and I got you pregnant in order to keep it? My dastardly deeds astound me. But like father like son, I expect. Clearly such wicked exploitation of women runs in my family. Look at the unspeakable antics of Sir George, back in the sixteenth century.'

'But I thought you were different . . .' As she said it, she realised that it belied her claim of premeditated vengeance.

'Big mistake,' he mocked, sliding his hand from her nape down to the button appliqué of her white sweatshirt, tracing the tender swell of her breast with ruthless possessiveness. 'Bad blood never changes. Besides, from what you've told me this morning, you came to Fleetwood Manor to see what you could get out of the

Fleetwoods. When you found you weren't Sir Robert's bastard daughter, you married me with a view to avenging your mother's honour. Or is that putting too melodramatic an interpretation on the matter? Which is the truth, Emma? Did you marry me out of some kind of conspiracy? Or did you marry me because you couldn't resist my wealth and charm?'

'I *hate* you...' she breathed involuntarily, shuddering as his seeking fingers moved lower, cupped her swollen breast gently, his thumb rotating against the jut of the nipple with patient skill. 'God, Dominick, I hate you...'

'So I gather,' he murmured, moving abruptly to trap her against the pillows, his mouth thinning. 'But love and hate can be interchangeable, I've heard, especially in bed...'

'No...' She'd meant it to be a sharp rebuff. Instead, it was a panic-stricken moan, huskier than she'd intended. Her traitorous body was already clamouring for his physical touch, even as her pride winced at his dominance.

'Don't worry,' he soothed sardonically, tugging the sweatshirt up and flicking open the wispy blue lace bra, 'I won't do anything to hurt you, my vengeful little bride. But I'm entitled to examine the receptacle of my future progeny, am I not?'

'And I'm entitled to...to some privacy...' she hissed helplessly, writhing as he unzipped her jeans, peeled them down, undressed her like a reluctant doll. 'To some privacy and respect...'

'As my bride,' he assured her, kissing the words into her throat with a force which shook her, before lifting his dark head once more, 'you're entitled to my name, my house, my lands, and my money, sweet Emma. And I, surely, am entitled to conjugal rights as old as time itself...'

'Haven't you heard of the new law?' It was a desperate threat, she knew, and doomed to failure. 'Marital rape exists now, you know...!'

'*Rape*?' he mocked, his voice thickening. He hauled her flat on the covers, and ran skilled, tantalising fingers the length of her body, then leaned back to inspect her with a blaze of male arrogance which took her breath away. 'I may be one of your despised Fleetwood males, my sweet, submissive wife, but I assure you rape has never been one of my vices...'

She gave an involuntary gasp as he smoothed his hands up to the peaks of her breasts, bent to suckle each nipple with implacable determination. She clenched her fists in anguish as his tongue flickered arousingly at the taut, rosy tips until she felt herself contract inwardly with the piercing shafts of longing.

'Dominick, you don't *own* me...' she sobbed as with infinite care he smoothed exploratory hands over the still smooth silk of her stomach, caressed the vulnerable softness of her thighs. It was useless to pretend, she realised bleakly. Their passion-drowned week in Athens had left her defenceless against his knowledge of her responses, his methodical voyage of discovery of every inch, every nerve-ending, every erogenous zone her body could conceivably possess.

'Don't I?' he taunted huskily, watching her convulse beneath his intimate onslaught. 'This marriage may have turned sour overnight, my darling, but we belong together, you and I.'

'Dominick...'

'Just say the word, sweetheart...do you want me?'

'No...!'

'You're lying,' he teased mockingly. 'Tell the truth, Emma...' He'd discarded his own clothes, manoeuvred himself between her tense, trembling legs, and with audacious confidence he dropped his head to the soft dark curls at the apex of her thighs, let his tongue explore the hot secrets of her femininity as she fought to control her desire. '*My* baby...' he whispered, raising his dark head with an abrupt flash of ferocious emotion which caught her breath. His fingers clenched around her hipbones, his thumbs smoothing the silky hollow of her groin. Dropping his head again, he traced a line of hungry kisses across the line of her pelvic floor, with a primitive, masculine claim to the delicate mystery within. '*My* child growing inside you, Emma...don't even *think* of leaving, with my baby inside you...'

'I'll do whatever I want...' she choked, finding strength from somewhere to challenge his arrogant command. 'And it's *my* child just as much as yours!'

'So much hatred,' he taunted roughly, his hands moulding her body, invading and boldly conquering, until she felt the tremors of sexual desire mounting higher and higher. His hard strength, his muscled weight as he pinned her to the bed, his arrogant skill as he drove her, again and again, to the peak of fulfillment and then drew back, whittled away her defences. Finally she couldn't think or reason; the physical need for him blotted out her intellect.

'Tell me you want me, Emma...' The order was a hoarse groan as he poised above her, a wall of muscle and sinew, holding himself in check with flinty control.

'God help me, yes...*yes*...!' Unbelievably, infuriatingly, the furious sob was torn from her throat as her senses melted and dissolved into surrender. His blue eyes smokily triumphant, he thrust inside her. The sensation, the combination of fury and desire, love and hate, was explosive. He filled her so completely that she shut her eyes and dug her nails into his shoulders, clinging to him as if her very life depended on it...

'Oh, Emma...' The breathed words were like a ragged caress against her lips. The rhythm of love, the surge of possession, the bitter ecstasy of their physical compatibility, rushed up like a hot invisible flood, and drowned her like a tidal wave. She gasped, heard her voice moaning his name. She felt incoherent and mindless, and so utterly routed in the sordid fight that she hardly believed it all possible when the fires died down, and the heat cooled a little, and she found herself cradled none too gently in the arms of a man who didn't love her...

Not only a man who didn't love her, she added bitterly to herself, but a man who had tricked her into marrying him to gain his inheritance, and whose child she now carried, tiny and unformed, in the fragile safety of her womb...

'I think you'd better tell me all about what my father did to your mother,' Dominick informed her easily, across the dinner-table. 'I'd like to be well-informed about the charges against me.'

She lifted her eyes from her blank study of her plate. Since Dominick's dramatic victory earlier, they'd skirted each other with almost elaborate politeness. The tension in the air was so potent, she imagined that a lighted match might cause an explosion.

With a slight shrug, she said lightly, 'You know your father was a philandering womaniser. You told me so yourself...'

'True. But I was blissfully ignorant about his seduction of your mother.'

She felt her face colour under that mocking regard. In casual dark green silk shirt and charcoal trousers, Dominick looked controlled, elegant, undeniably powerful. Lord of his manor. Smug victor, triumphant winner of his cruel little inheritance game...

'You needn't make it sound so... trivial,' she said softly. 'My parents had a happy marriage...'

'That's why your mother went to bed with my father, is it? Maybe I should be relieved that my marriage is turning out remarkably *unhappy*?'

His biting sarcasm made her flinch. She watched him lift the wine bottle, pour more of the vintage Médoc into her glass. She picked it up with nerveless fingers, and stared at it. It shone blood-red in the candlelight. Mrs Shields had come up with a feast fit for kings tonight, maybe urged on to improve the deadly atmosphere enveloping the manor, like a poison cloud descending on everyone. The asparagus soup, the beautifully cooked beef Wellington, the tender home-grown broccoli and carrots did nothing to ease the mood of wary bitterness in the big, dark-panelled dining-room.

'I'm sure that my mother wasn't entirely innocent,' she conceded quietly, 'but my father was being treated for depression. He...he...well, I gather from what was said that he must have lost his...'

'Sex drive?' Dominick suggested coolly.

'Yes. It does happen to men sometimes. And that must have made him even more depressed. It put a strain on the marriage...'

Dominick's gaze was blandly curious across the table.

'What a heart-rending tale. Let me guess—your mother found satisfaction in the arms of my father, then wondered why her marriage broke up when her affair came to light?'

'It's easy to sneer!' she shot back shakily. She should know better by now than to let Dominick goad her. But she was painfully aware that in the telling the story gave scant respect to her mother's morals. 'Everyone makes mistakes!'

'They do indeed.' Dominick's gaze didn't leave her face, but she thought he suddenly looked gauntly angry. A muscle twitched slightly in the hard line of his jaw, but apart from that he looked as if he was carved in stone.

'The way I see it,' he went on, after another long pause, 'is that neither your mother nor my father comes out of that saga very well . . .'

'I *know*,' she said raggedly. She dropped her fork back on her plate, and took a shaky drink of wine. 'Do you think I can't *see* that? The whole thing stinks; nobody behaved well! I've been feeling confused about the whole thing ever since my father told me, before he died.'

'We don't choose our parents. We don't necessarily inherit their faults. And what about your melodramatic revenge?' he probed softly. 'I thought you blamed the wicked Fleetwoods? Intended to make me pay for the damage?'

His eyes held a trace of mockery, but there was a gentleness in his deep voice which made her heart squeeze in anguish. 'Or was that something you threw at me on the spur of the moment, Emma? Because your pride was wounded?'

She stared at him blindly.

'Why would you care, either way?' she whispered bitterly. 'Except that now, of course, I've managed to get pregnant. So I'm of value to you for different reasons...'

'Emma...' The controlled anger in his voice made her shiver slightly. 'Do you recall my telling you to trust me? If there's no trust between two people, there's no relationship worth speaking of. Wouldn't you agree?'

'I——'

'Yet the first moment I leave you alone you lose your trust in me. You accuse me of tricking you, you accuse me of using you——'

'So *I'm* in the wrong now?' she shot at him indignantly, although tears were choking the back of her throat. 'How convenient!'

'Worse still, you seem to be blindly judging me by the actions of my ancestors——'

'What about your family crest?' she taunted unevenly. '*More majorum*? After the manner of our ancestors?'

'So I should judge you to be like your mother?' he countered calmly and coldly. 'Maybe I'd better make quite sure I steer clear of depression at any cost? Or maybe I should watch you and young Jamie like a hawk from now on?'

The colour flashed to the roots of her hair at the icy distaste in his voice. Misery descended like a lead weight inside her. Slowly, with as much dignity as she could manage, she stood up.

'Yes. Maybe you should,' she tossed at him in a tightly suppressed voice, 'although frankly you won't have to watch either of us much longer, Dominick. I can't stay here in this atmosphere.

It's not good for my baby. I'll pack my things and leave, first thing in the morning, and get myself a good *lawyer* . . .' She caught the flare of cold fury in his eyes, and added quickly, 'And no amount of your . . . your high-handed bullying tactics can stop me!'

CHAPTER EIGHT

A BRILLIANT May sunshine mocked her the following morning. But at least it brought a ray of warmth into the otherwise bleak landscape of her life, Emma thought unhappily. She moved like a zombie around her bedroom, the one she'd locked herself securely into last night. In the event, Dominick hadn't even tried the doorhandle, she realised with a sharp twinge of irony. Had he given up on her? Realised there was nothing he could say to excuse himself for his underhand trick over the will?

She could believe it more easily if it weren't for her pregnancy. What was it he'd said? Don't even *think* of leaving, with my baby inside you...

She shivered convulsively, pressing her things down hard into the suitcase. There were other things in the big wardrobes in Dominick's room. The room they'd shared since Dominick had asked her to marry him. She'd leave them there. This morning, early, was her chosen time to leave. All she had to do was walk downstairs, ask Jamie to fetch her cases, get into her little red Renault, and drive away. Cathy's flat was only fifteen miles away. She'd borrow a sleeping-bag on the sofa for a few nights, until she made some plans. It was as simple as that. There need be no great drama, no struggle for control. She was a grown woman, with her own mind. If she wanted to leave, she could leave ...

These silent reassurances did little to help, as she ventured into the bathroom and silently slid the bolt home on Dominick's connecting door. Like a guilty thief, she showered and dried herself and slipped out, unlocking Dominick's door and running for the sanctuary of her own room like someone pursued by demons. There was no sound from Dominick. An ominous lack of re-action of any kind ...

Dressing shakily in white body, denim jeans and a loose ice-grey silk shirt she'd bought in Athens, she pushed her feet into soft tan suede boots and brushed her hair into a shiny curtain around her shoulders. Her face shimmered in the mirror, pale as a ghost's. She thought fleetingly of the story Dominick had told her, about the bones in the secret chamber, the tales of ghostly shapes along the attic landing. She'd spent a couple of hours up there last night, driven by a dogged sense of professionalism to put her work in order, to annotate her findings so far for a future archivist. Shivering in the chilly darkness, with only the gas lamp and the hissing Calor-gas fire for company, she'd felt uneasily conscious of those silly stories ... maybe because she'd half feared that Dominick would appear at any second, and force another confrontation ...

It was too early to bother Mrs Shields or Jamie, she decided, taking her cases down to the hall

herself. Escape proved depressingly easy, after all.
The house was silent, the hall deserted. Her car
started, her exit down the crunching driveway of
the manor uninterrupted. When she got out on
the open road, she had to pull in to the nearest
layby, until the tears stopped streaming down her
face, blinding her completely...

'Telephone for you, Emm.' Cathy, who'd rushed
to the phone hoping it was Tobias, came back
into the sitting-room of her small flat and gave
Emma an apologetic grin. 'It's Dominick. Didn't
take him long to track you down! He must have
rung Tobias for my number...'

'Tell him I don't want to speak to him,' she
pleaded, beginning to tremble all over. This was
ridiculous. How could a simple telephone call
seem so threatening?

Cathy resolutely shook her head. 'Nope. He
said it was urgent. I think you should see what
he wants.'

Dominick's deep voice, even on the other end
of the telephone, sounded so belovedly familiar
that Emma had to bite her lip to stop herself from
bursting into foolish tears.

'Yes?'

'Well done,' he said abruptly. 'You've surprised me, Emma. As revenge, it was pretty neat.'

She stared at the garishly patterned carpet in
Cathy's hallway. The flat was rented furnished,
since Cathy had only recently come to the area

to take up her new job, teaching history to eleven-year-olds at the local private girls' school.

'I'm not sure what you're talking about...' she began stiffly. Dominick's curt laugh silenced her.

'No? You mean you know nothing about any fire in the attic?' he barked coldly.

'*What*? Dominick, I——'

'Leaving the Calor-gas heater too close to the archives? Sending priceless Fleetwood family records up in smoke? Nearly burning down the whole goddamned bloody manor house in the process?'

The hall had begun to sway ominously. Conscious of her unfamiliar reaction to receiving unpleasant shocks, in her newly pregnant state, she groped blindly for the chair and collapsed on to it.

'Dominick ... you can't be *serious*?' It was a breathed prayer, a plea for this to be a sick, cruel joke.

'Never more so, my sweet-tempered bride.'

'You can't ... you can't possibly think I would do such a thing ...? Surely you couldn't believe that of me ...?'

Cathy, drawn by the agonised sound of Emma's voice, had stopped her Saturday morning dusting session and come into the hall, her eyes troubled.

There was a brief silence at Dominick's end. Then he cursed unrepeatably at the other end of the line.

'You're right,' he snapped icily, 'I can't quite believe it of you. But I suggest you get yourself back here in under an hour and try convincing me of your innocence, *Lady* Fleetwood. Or I might feel compelled to think the worst.'

She drew in a short, furious breath.

'Is this *blackmail*?' she hissed. 'I come back straight away, or you blame me for the fire? Is that it? I'm beginning to wonder if you started the damn fire yourself, Dominick!'

'Be careful, Emma,' he advised her quietly. 'Don't push me too much further or I won't be responsible for what happens...'

'Dominick, for God's sake...'

'If you're the dedicated archivist you claim to be, you'll get back here right now and review the scene of destruction.'

'Yes,' she said grimly. 'Yes. I'll come back. Straight away. And this might sound a silly thing to say, but whatever you do don't let anyone throw *anything* away...'

Cathy took one look at her white, stricken face, and insisted on driving.

'You look ghastly,' she told Emma cheerfully, bundling her into the passenger seat of her battered Volkswagen. 'You'd be a danger to the public...'

'Thanks,' Emma said bleakly, trying to smile. It was all she managed to say during the drive back to Fleetwood Manor. The fire-engine was coming out of the manor-house drive as they approached. Emma felt her stomach plunge, apprehension gripping her. All that historical detail . . . all those wonderful old records . . . She felt a wave of disbelief and sadness engulf her. And anger—how could Dominick think she'd deliberately started the fire? But how could she have been so stupid . . . so irresponsible as to have left the Calor-gas heater on all night?

Dominick came to the door as they stopped. In Levis, leather boots and denim shirt, his black hair tousled in the wind, he looked so tough, uncompromising and darkly forbidding, and Cathy gave her a quick, reassuring squeeze on the arm.

'Heathcliff awaits,' she teased lightly. 'Want me to stay for moral support, love?'

Emma shook her head. 'You'd better not. No point getting caught in the cross-fire . . .'

She stepped numbly out of the car and waited until her friend had driven off before turning to face Dominick.

'Is it *all* ruined?' It was an anguished question as she met his cold gaze. 'Are all the old papers burned, Dominick?'

'Some survived,' he said shortly, raking a brief glance over her before turning towards the entrance. 'Luckily it looks as though you'd tidied most of it away into the storage boxes and metal caskets. But it's one hell of a mess up there . . .'

'Dominick, if I inadvertently caused the fire,' she began painfully, 'I'm sorry. I . . . I can't tell you how sorry I am. I can't believe I could have been so careless. I . . . I was feeling preoccupied last night, for obvious reasons, but——'

'Let's just say the balance of your mind was temporarily disturbed,' he mocked softly. Casting a quick look at him, she couldn't decipher his mood at all. Was he still suspicious that she might have started the fire as revenge?

'Believe me, I'd rather...rather chop off my right arm than set fire to something like that!' she whispered urgently. 'I...I would never stoop so low! You have to believe me, Dominick! Surely you know me well enough?'

'Why the hell should I believe anything you say? I've only known you a few weeks,' he pointed out ruthlessly, escorting her up to the attics. 'We hardly know each other at all, do we, Emma, darling? We've both been hiding so many nasty secrets from each other, nothing we discover should surprise us, should it?'

The acrid smell of smoke hit her as she reached the top of the narrow stairway. The damage was worsened considerably by the gallons of water pumped in by the firemen. As Dominick had said, it was a mess. She could hardly bring herself to pick among the debris.

'Were...were you insured?'

'God knows.' Dominick raked a hand through his black hair, his gaze bleak. 'What's money compared with hundreds of years of historical records?'

'I know...' She started to lift a box from the floor, and he gave a muffled curse and lunged down to stop her.

'Jamie and a couple of estate workers are coming to carry everything down to the study. I don't want you lifting anything...'

She straightened up slowly, meeting his eyes. Her heart contracted foolishly in her chest. It wasn't *her* he was concerned for, it was the baby she was carrying inside her. She knew that. But even so the flash of concern had caught her on the raw.

'I'm not ill,' she said quietly, 'I'm pregnant, that's all...'

'My mother had complications when she had me,' he retorted coolly, 'and you fainted yesterday.'

'But I'm perfectly healthy and normal. *Your* mother's gynaecological problems are hardly anything to do with me!'

'I'm not taking any chances.'

'I'll do my best to ensure that *our* baby is born healthy and full-term,' she agreed stiffly.

'So you'll stay?' His voice was harshly bleak. 'You won't run out on me again, Emma?'

'So you can run regular health-checks on the mother-to-be? Make sure your possible son and heir has the right ante-natal care? That's all that matters to you, isn't it?'

'You know bloody well it isn't!' The cold growl of fury made her catch her breath.

'Oh, right, I forgot. Keeping up appearances of being happily married is important as well, is it? Does that have an influence on your inheritance as well? If your new bride walks out within a month, do you stand to lose out again?'

'I thought Vanessa Buckingham was the bitch,' he murmured through his teeth, 'but you'd win any contest, Emma.'

Hot tears stung her eyes, but she furiously blinked them away.

'I'll stay,' she said in a low, shaky voice, 'at least until the damaged records have been sorted out. That's the least I can do, since it was all my fault... But don't expect me to like being here! How did you *imagine* I'd feel, when I found out why you'd rushed to marry me? And... and *impregnate* me,' she shot back shakily. 'Or did you think I'd be so grateful for being Lady Fleetwood that I'd forgive you anything? Lowly gamekeeper's daughter makes it to the top of the social scale, et cetera?'

He'd caught hold of her shoulders, and gave her a short, brutal shake.

'I expected you to trust me,' he ground out angrily, his eyes burning hers with a fierce emotion which shook her to the core. 'Just as I was prepared to trust you. But it seems you'd rather believe I'm a liar. So what's to stop me believing the same of you?'

Releasing her abruptly, he steered her back towards the stairs. A hard lump of misery was threatening to choke her as she walked silently ahead of him. She no longer knew what to think, she realised wearily. What to believe...

* * *

The weekend passed in a blur of salvaging as much as possible of the records. Jamie and two other estate workers manhandled everything down from the attics, and stacked it in the study. Emma found herself trapped back at Fleetwood Manor, by her own guilty conscience. The precarious state of her marriage, and the hostile atmosphere with Dominick, made things unbearably tense. But she couldn't even consider leaving again. Not until she'd done what she could to make amends for her careless mistake with the fire. She worked for hours on end, sifting meticulously through the records, separating the irrevocably charred from the water-damaged, and the partly legible. She talked to the insurance assessors, she organised assistance from the local history society, she enlisted the support of as many people as she could muster. But privately she could have wept at the disaster she'd unwittingly caused.

Dominick was nowhere to be found as she drank endless cups of tea and worked doggedly on. Presumably he'd gone off to his country club, she decided. He was probably unwinding, the way he liked to at weekends. Only this time he was most likely playing tennis and swimming with Vanessa, she thought acidly. Had he told Vanessa about the pregnancy? Were they exulting in the sheer stroke of good fortune? Marvelling perhaps at Dominick's sexual potency...?

The organisers of the charity ball milled about the manor house, while Emma stayed ensconced in the study. She could hear drifts of voices, faint hammering, the clattering of equipment and furniture moving going on in the distance. Mrs Shields, delivering the sandwich supper Emma had requested, confided that tickets had been put at a three-figure sum, and the ball was sold out. The possibility of extra interest, aroused by the newspaper reports of the mystery new Lady Fleetwood, might have caused the run on tickets.

'Surely not,' Emma breathed, gazing at the housekeeper with horrified eyes. 'You mean I'll be on show, some kind of... of circus freak?'

Mrs Shields laughed. 'Goodness me, no. You're a beauty, my dear, and you surely know it. Just like your mother. I was terribly fond of Amy Stuart, you know. I was very sorry about what happened... sorry when they left.'

'Do you know why they left?' Emma heard the words come out, and could have bitten off her tongue. But the gleam in Mrs Shields's eyes revealed prior knowledge.

'As a matter of fact, there's not a lot I don't know about the Fleetwoods, dear.'

Emma felt her breath catch in her chest.

'You knew... about my mother and... and Sir Robert—their affair?'

'Sir Robert *adored* your mother. Lady Fleetwood stepped in and gave him an ultimatum. There was a row to end all rows, I can tell you. That's why your parents had to leave. If Sir Robert had had his way, he'd have divorced and married Amy Stuart. She was the love of his life, dear, that's the truth ... but there was no affair. Sir Robert respected Amy too much to make love to her while they were both tied to other partners.' Mrs Shields sighed. 'Unfortunately, neither Lady Fleetwood nor your father would agree to a divorce. Which left four very unhappy people ...'

When Mrs Shields had gone, Emma sat for a long time, staring at the pile of papers in front of her. It wasn't so surprising, after all, that Mrs Shields should know what went on in such intimate detail. Did that mean she knew precisely what was going on between Dominick and herself now? Emma felt herself wince inwardly. Jamie would have told his grandmother, anyway. There was very little privacy in this kind of situation ...

Rubbing her forehead distractedly, she tried to think straight. She wasn't sure if the information she'd just been given made things better or worse. Possibly just a fraction better, Emma conceded, sucking the stem of her reading glasses, and unhooking her ankle from her chair-leg. At least it put Sir Robert in a slightly warmer, a slightly more *human* light. What a disaster it was to be too partisan. To take sides over something she had no way of fully understanding ... For the first time in her memory, she began to see that there had been more than one side to the sad little tale her father had so bitterly related ... No wonder her woolly notions of blame and revenge had been so vague and unformed. When it came to her mother and Sir Robert Fleetwood, who could say which of the two had been more to blame?

Carefully and methodically she put her work away, checked meticulously that every lamp and switch was off, and went up to her bedroom. Sleepiness had overtaken her, with a strange abruptness she'd noticed since she'd been pregnant. She felt so sleepy, she could almost have dozed off with her head on the desk in the study. Bed was a luxurious prospect. But first she needed a hot bath. A long, lazy soak in fragrant bubbles. Walking like a sleepwalker into the bathroom, clad only in her white towelling bathrobe, she stopped in dismay.

Dominick was relaxing lazily in the bath, apparently indifferent to the bubbles lapping over the edge and soaking the floor. There was a whisky glass on the table beside him. An inch of whisky remained. He gave her a dangerous smile which almost stopped her heartbeat.

'Ah, my devoted bride. How thoughtful,' he murmured lightly. 'Have you come to scrub my back?'

Backing hastily out, she knocked her elbow hard against the door-jamb, and gave a yelp of pain. To her alarm, Dominick had nonchalantly stood up, water streaming off the iron-hard planes of his body, supremely unselfconscious as he stepped out of the bath and came towards her. Throat dry, heart thumping, she felt riveted to the spot.

'Don't look so virginally shocked, Lady Fleetwood, darling,' he drawled mockingly. The threatening glitter in his eyes had intensified. 'It takes more than half a measure of whisky to make me drunk, if that's what's upsetting you. And we *are* married.'

'Really? So where've you been all weekend?', she whispered, her eyes on the width of his chest, the droplets of water trickling down through the sprinkle of dark hair between flat brown nipples. Unable to resist the lure, she followed the drops down to the ridge of muscle in his diaphragm, the dark arrow of hair down the centre of his flat stomach to the even darker masculine threat below. She felt her own stomach clench in response.

'Where do you imagine I've been?' he goaded softly, watching her like a predatory hawk.

'With Vanessa?' she suggested tightly.

'Well, of course——' the deep voice was biting '—with Vanessa. Who else knows the legal complexities of my inheritance in such depth and detail?' He flicked a towel from the free-standing wooden towel-horse, and wrapped it carelessly around his hips.

She turned to go back to her room, blindly furious, but he caught her upper arm.

'Where are you going?' he teased lightly. 'You look in need of a hot bath, Emma.'

'I don't want to share a bath with you,' she managed in a choked voice. 'Let me go, Dominick...'

'Not just yet.' He drew her round to smooth
the robe from her shoulders, letting it fall to the
cork-tiled floor at their feet. 'You didn't mind
sharing my bath in Athens...'

'That was different...'

'The honeymoon's over, of course,' he agreed,
a steely note of humour making her blush bright
red. 'All right, sweet Emma, you can have the
bath all to yourself...'

Without warning he bent to pick her up, and
deposited her in the warm bubbles. Pride told
her she should immediately scramble out and
defend herself, but physical tiredness, the heat of
the water, and the dark glitter in Dominick's blue
eyes as he knelt down beside her, sponge in hand,
seemed to fill her with a kind of resigned lethargy
and languor. His mouth twisting as he noted her
passive reaction, he soaped the sponge, took hold
of one of her hands and slowly smoothed it up
over the slender length of her arm, across the
hollow of her throat, and then down purposefully and with consummate arrogance, over the
full globes of her breasts, where they bobbed
vulnerably just beneath the bubbly surface of the
water.

In spite of the rift between them, the heat of
desire flickered uncontrollably inside her. How
did he know exactly how to arouse her, every
time, with such devilish accuracy?

Heat engulfing her, she closed her eyes, gritting
her teeth as, with great care and thoroughness,
Dominick slid the soapy sponge lower, reaching

his other hand into the water, sliding it between her knees. Her legs felt weightless in the deep water. Her ability to resist was severely hampered by the slipperiness of the bath. And besides, resistance was out of the question now, because with expert care he was lightly stroking the sponge against the delicate, most intimate part of her body where an invisible energy seemed to be gathering and expanding, regardless of pride or common sense...

'We have to take great care of you.' His deep, taunting voice sounded thicker as his exploration grew bolder. 'Now that you're creating a new little life inside you, Emma, darling...'

Squirming helplessly, she realised that he'd abandoned the sponge. The hard male fingers soaping in intimate places were audaciously inquisitive. And hopelessly arousing.

'You might only be a few weeks pregnant, but your body's changing already,' he murmured huskily, cupping the swell of her breasts, bending to lick his tongue experimentally around the darkening aureoles, darting impossibly exciting feelings right down to her groin. 'Your breasts are fuller. Your skin feels different. You feel different here...and here...' His seeking fingers probed between her thighs again, demandingly sure, driving her wild with need. 'You're incredibly sexy anyway, Emma, but you're even sexier pregnant...'

Opening her mouth to speak, she found her lips trapped and covered by Dominick's hard mouth. His tongue drove powerfully against hers, mimicking the act of lovemaking, making her senses swim.

'Oh, Dominick...' It was half-sob, half muffled protest, half despairing surrender against his invading kiss, and his invading, demanding caresses. 'How can I want you so much, when I *hate* you so much?'

His answer was to lift her abruptly out of the bath, carry her streaming with water to the wide bed in his room, and take her, without further foreplay, and with such suppressed anger in his primitive, almost brutal thrusts of possession that she shuddered with tears even as she convulsed with helpless fulfilment...

His easy victory haunted her over the next few days. He'd gone back to London, to more court appearances, more time with his colleague Vanessa? Emma didn't know. She tried to convince herself she didn't care. But she did. She cared so much, she felt as if she was slowly breaking apart with the intensity of her feelings. Whatever the truth of their marriage, she loved him. Deeply, totally, in a way she'd never loved anyone else in her life. When he walked into a room, her heart leaped. When he left, she felt as if the sun vanished, the world went grey. The humiliation of feeling like this, when she'd been a pawn in his game to inherit, was almost intolerable...

The May Ball preparations were nearly complete. The Great Hall was transformed into a fairy-tale ballroom, festooned with intricate swags of leaves and flowers. The theme of peach and cream and pale green lent the medieval hall a freshness which Emma found entrancing. The minstrels' gallery would hold the band. Caterers had bustled around putting up long, white-clothed trestle-tables, complete with elegant floral centrepieces. Emma, in her new position as Lady Fleetwood, found herself being consulted on a variety of matters from the viability of fresh strawberries to the provision of non-alcoholic punch. These were mere formalities, she knew. The charity ball committee was made up of extremely capable ladies who'd organised this particular ball since time immemorial. She suspected that her curiosity value was largely to blame for this sudden need to confer with the lady of the house...

Saturday was a warm, sunny day. The kind of mystical May day which banished all memory of a chilly English winter. Fleetwood Manor basked in its ancient splendour, its gardens abruptly flowering into a mass of crimson and mauve rhododendrons in the unfamiliar heat. It would be a good day for the ball, she thought. Guests would be able to spill out into the grounds, cool off after the dancing, breathe in the unforgettable scents of the honeysuckle in the courtyard behind the Great Hall...

Whether it was the lovely day, or a degree of acceptance triggered by her delicate condition, Emma found herself feeling a little more mellow. By early evening, she'd showered and washed her hair, laid out her dress on the bed, pinned her hair into an elegant chestnut topknot, and made up her face with a hand which shook with nerves. Dominick had still not come back from London. But she had no doubt that he would make it. The appearance of Sir Dominick and Lady Fleetwood at the ball was of prime importance. The villagers, the local VIPs, a sprinkling of the county's aristocracy plus a fair proportion of London socialites were apparently waiting with baited breath to see the new couple in public together for the first time.

Immature notions of revenge were quickly dismissed. She had to put on a respectable performance as Dominick's adoring new bride... Panic returned like a clench of pain in her stomach. Could she go through with it? Long-term, their marriage was doomed, she knew. Short-term... as long as he treated her with reasonable respect, she told herself with bitter irony, she'd be all right...

Smoothing a hint of heather-pink lipstick over the fullness of her mouth, brushing a feather-light puff of blusher on the pale oval of her cheeks, she tried to boost her confidence. She rarely wore much make-up. The effect tonight was surprisingly enhancing. Perhaps Dominick was right. His theory that her skin glowed with pregnancy, that she radiated some new quality which altered her appearance...

She wriggled into the full-length sheath of her dress, and stepped back from the cheval-mirror to check the fit. Thankfully it was too early for her pregnancy to show. The slinky-cut fabric clung to the slender curves of her figure, the grey silk shot subtly through with green and silver, making a shimmering tube of a dress, high at the front, scooping daringly low at the back. Dominick had lounged in a chair in the evening-wear department at Harrods, while she'd tried on half a dozen gowns. This had been his choice...and she had to admit she wouldn't have had the confidence to choose it for herself.

A car door slammed on the sweep of the drive below, the heavy, familiar clunk of the Porsche's door. Dominick was back. With a foolish twinge of anticipation, she went to the window, gazed down into the evening sunshine. Then her stomach sank.

Dominick, tall and dark in his smart London suit, was stepping out of his car. Vanessa's XR3 had drawn up beside him, and the blonde was sliding out, laughing up at him. She was already dressed for the ball, and she looked stunning in a red strapless ballgown, cinched at her tiny waist, frothing out to mid-calf length in luxurious layers of taffeta. She was with one of the charity ball committee members. Presumably, she'd arrived early, to help with last-minute arrangements...

Dominick turned to speak to them. The other woman went on ahead, and Vanessa's hand smoothed his arm in an unmistakably possessive, flirtatious gesture. They walked together towards the entrance, Vanessa's arm clinging triumphantly to Dominick's.

Emma closed her eyes, thoughts of a tolerable evening vanishing in the rush of pain and anger. How dared he? How *could* he arrive with Vanessa?

She turned away and went to sit on the bed. She tried to stay calm. She tried to keep cool. But she felt as if she could erupt with the force of her emotions. The fury burned through her, like a lighted taper towards a cache of explosives . . .

CHAPTER NINE

'ENJOYING the ball, Lady Fleetwood?' Dominick's mocking murmur in her ear made her stiffen with suppressed anger. The strain of looking happy, when all she wanted to do was strangle him, was getting too much.

'Sorry,' she retorted in a low, bitter voice. 'Am I letting my cheerful mask slip?'

'Only slightly. You resemble Anne Boleyn just before Henry sent her to the block. Was the meal not to your liking, my dear?'

His cool drawl was maddening. She pleated the damask tablecloth with her fingers, and desperately tried not to think about being the centre of attention. It was difficult. Not only was she an object of frank curiosity, as the new Lady Fleetwood, but she was wearing the diamond choker and earrings that Dominick had given her when he'd finished dressing for the evening. Their blatant value sparkled in every perfectly cut stone. 'You may not want them,' he'd taunted ruthlessly, fastening the double-stranded choker at her nape with cool fingers, making her shiver with furious awareness, 'but we have to keep up appearances tonight, don't we, darling?'

They'd eaten a superb meal of lemon sole, chicken *Véronique*, and fresh strawberries and

167

cream. The wine was flowing, the band was playing faintly in the background. They were sitting at the centre of the top table, with chatter and laughter and clinking of glasses all around them. Cathy and Tobias were the only allies she could see amid a mass of strange faces. And further down the table, talking and joking confidently with her dinner companion, was Vanessa. The blonde girl's eyes seemed to stray towards them far too often for Emma's peace of mind. She could feel the simmering resentment fighting to the surface. It took all her control to smile sweetly at her husband as he refilled her glass with Médoc.

'Maybe I'm just wondering when, like Anne Boleyn, I'm going to be conveniently disposed of,' she countered tautly. 'After all, Sir George was rumoured to have done away with that poor governess he seduced, wasn't he? And don't forget your family crest—*more majorum*?'

Dominick leaned back in his chair, his eyes gleaming. He looked magnificent in his dinner-jacket and bow-tie. His curly black hair was slicked back under ruthless control. His skin looked dusky against the dazzling white of his dress-shirt. She took a deep breath, and averted her eyes.

'That story was pure romantic conjecture.' Dominick grinned. 'Although I've often wondered if Sir George locked the poor soul in the priest hole and conveniently forgot her. Hence the pile of bones someone found a few hundred years later.'

'You would find such a story amusing,' she snapped softly. 'So am I going to disappear soon? After the baby is born, perhaps? So you can eventually marry your beloved Vanessa?'

Dominick's smile had hardened. He took her left hand, grasping it a little too tight for comfort as he inspected the rings on her finger.

'Don't you think you're taking this wronged-wife act of yours a little too far, Emma?' His soft reprimand was like a red rag to her suppressed fury. 'We're living in the twentieth century, not acting out some gothic horror story, darling.'

'How could you spend so much time talking to Vanessa Buckingham tonight?' she hissed, past caring who heard them. 'Unless you take a sadistic delight in rubbing salt into wounds?'

'And has it occurred to you that maybe——' he caught her tense hand and lifted it to his lips, kissing the back of her knuckles with wry mockery '—maybe the wounds are self-inflicted, Emma?'

'You think you're so clever. The shrewd barrister who can side-step any straight question,' she whispered. 'But I just can't believe you can be so callous...'

'Hello there.' The female in question had come down the table to greet Emma with a cool smile. 'I hear congratulations are in order for a different reason this time!' Vanessa's green eyes were sweeping assessingly over Emma's slender figure in the silver-grey silk. 'You didn't waste much time, did you?'

Emma stiffened. Up till now, she'd managed to avoid any intimate conversation with Vanessa. She'd kept a smile on her lips, chatted politely to people who eyed her up and down with undisguised curiosity but a reasonable degree of respect. But all the time she'd been aware of Vanessa, smugly shadowing Dominick, skimming around flirtatiously in her scarlet dress, letting her tinkling laugh float across to Emma whenever she was in the vicinity... A surge of defiance made her shrug and smile casually.

'Dominick and I have a very...*highly sexed* relationship,' she murmured sweetly. 'I suppose a baby was...inevitable? And Dominick is thrilled to bits, aren't you, darling?'

There was an infinitesimal pause, before Dominick said with ominous blandness, 'Absolutely. Thrilled to bits.'

Vanessa's social smile had faded. The expression in the long green eyes was decidedly hostile. She straightened up as if she'd been slapped.

'I'm very happy for you,' she managed icily. She shot a thin smile at Dominick. His dark face was deadpan, but a gleam of unholy amusement shone in his eyes.

'Actually I've come to steal your husband away for a dance,' she added with a return of self-confidence, loudly enough for others to hear.

'Come on, Dominick, you know you waltz divinely!'

'How can I resist such flattery?' he said lazily. 'Excuse us, would you, darling?' To Emma's suppressed fury, he stood up and escorted Vanessa round to the dance-floor. For the next ten minutes she sat like a statue, feeling as if she'd been literally turned to stone. This was unbearable, she decided. No woman should be forced to endure the torment of watching her husband dancing with his mistress. The jealousy and anger reached bursting point by the time the couple returned to the table. Dominick looked darkly sardonic as he came back to her side. The look he skimmed over her was shuttered, but the gleam in his eyes as he drew her to her feet was unmistakable. Desire, she reflected, suppressing her outrage; he might not love her, but he found her sexually appealing. Was this to be her consolation?

'Now that I've demonstrated how well I can dance, would my beautiful, highly sexed little bride care to dance with me?' he murmured huskily, his heavy-lidded, teasing gaze bringing hot colour to her face.

The humiliations, the betrayals, the insults heaped on insults rose up in her throat, almost choking her with the surge of angry emotion.

Blindly she grasped her wine glass and, with a controlled shudder of fury, she flung the contents into his face.

'Go to hell, *Sir* Dominick!' she bit out. There was a sudden, shocked silence around them. Conversations ceased in mid-sentence. Quivering with rage and fear, she took in Dominick's motionless stance, the red wine forming a dark stain on the immaculate whiteness of his dress-shirt. The kindling fury she saw in his eyes was mixed with an amused glitter which fanned her indignation, made her heart pound even faster. He reached slowly into his breast pocket, extracted a large white handkerchief, and wiped the wine from his face. Taking her chance for escape, she darted quickly past him, and marched with commendable dignity from the hall. It took all her will-power not to run wildly away as if pursued by demons...

She should feel deeply ashamed for causing such a scene, she knew. But as she retreated upstairs and along the galleried landing she felt only a stubborn surge of satisfaction. Hugging her arms round herself, she headed for her room, then changed her mind. Dominick might come and find her there. He'd be angry, force a confrontation. She shivered at the thought. She might be high on a kind of adrenalin surge now, but she didn't relish the prospect of a fight with Dominick. Especially not the kind of fight he excelled at, one with sexual overtones which invariably sucked her down into the mire of desire and capitulation...

Hardly aware of her direction, she found herself climbing the stairs of the turret, to the old priest hole. There were dim wall-lights in the turret room, but the trap-door entrance gaped darkly as she pulled it up, the rope ladder dangling down and disappearing into the blackness.

The atmosphere down there came back to jog her memory. 'Centuries-old fear and anguish', she'd said to Dominick, and he'd laughed. A fresh wave of despair came over her. What had she done tonight? Tarnished the honour of the new baronet? Caused a scandal which would quite probably be all over town by tomorrow? Made a name for herself in the gossip columns already graced by Dominick's presence? She was certainly going to be repenting at leisure, she admitted. Bitter humour at the mess she'd got herself into threatened to turn into hysteria.

Twisting round, she grasped the rope ladder and began the descent into the confined area down below. She wasn't afraid of ghosts. And it wouldn't be all that dark once she got down there. The lights from the turret room would shine down, once her eyes got accustomed. The notion of going down there seemed oddly comforting, in her present emotional turmoil. She wanted to relive the sense of history she'd felt when she'd come down here with Dominick.

And while she wasn't going to admit to craving a hiding place from Dominick's wrath, she reflected, with a shiver, the notion of tucking herself away in the temporary safety of the priest hole did have certain attractions she couldn't, in all honesty, deny...

It was the dress which made her fall. Catching round the toe of her evening shoe, it threw her off balance. She missed her footing on the ladder, her fingers slipped on the rough rope, burning her, loosening her grip. In shocked silence, she plummeted downwards.

The impact numbed her. Winded, abruptly terrified for the baby, she lay there, slowly taking stock. She seemed to have survived the fall intact. Thank God for that, she told herself fervently. There were no ominous pains in her stomach, no nagging backache she'd read about which could signal imminent miscarriage. The pure relief put her muddled emotions in perspective. She might hate Dominick for betraying her trust, but she'd rather die than lose his baby... That simple, primitive knowledge somehow made her feel better...

She sat very still while she recovered from the fall. The only sounds were her own laboured breathing and the rapid thudding of her heart. It was pounding so loudly in the small enclosure, the beat sounded deafening.

What a feather-brained idiot she was... The stupidity, the sheer, mind-numbing childishness of climbing down here, hit her as forcibly as the impact of her landing. She groaned aloud, half laughing, half tearful. If this was the best she could do to assert herself, she might as well call it a day, she flayed herself silently. If Lady

Fleetwood was going to throw glasses of wine at her new husband and lord of the manor in full view of an important social gathering, the least she could do was show a little courage in the aftermath...

She'd go back and find him. Have the final confrontation if necessary. Anything but hide in this dark little priest hole like a naughty child in disgrace...

Resolutely she turned on to her hands and knees, and began to stand up. Pain shot through her, and she collapsed with a gasp. Her left ankle was twisted, or sprained. There was no way she could climb out.

Sitting back down, her eyes becoming accustomed to the dark, she tried to see the funny side. There certainly was one. In black comedy terms, at any rate. She could see the headlines, if the newspapers got hold of the story. 'New Lady Fleetwood throws wine in husband's face, hides in priest hole to escape retribution...'

The minutes ticked by. After a while the silence became unbearable. And the thought came to her with a sickening lurch...who would think of looking for her here?

Dominick might imagine she'd rushed to her room, then he might suspect that she'd gone off in her car. After that, he might search any other room in the house, or the garden...but why, in the name of heaven, would he imagine for one outlandish moment that his wife was languishing at the bottom of the priest hole in the turret?

She shivered as the past use of the hiding place came creeping back to mind, the terror and loneliness of those long-ago fugitives... the melodramatic tale of Sir George and his governess...

It was going to be a long night, she realised nervously. In fact, she accepted, shivering again with sudden cold as the chill of the old walls closed in around her, it could be even longer than that. She'd just have to keep shouting. Feeling utterly ridiculous, she began to call Dominick's name...

It was only a couple of hours before rescue came. It had felt like days. She might loathe her new husband, she told herself weakly, but when he appeared at the trap-door she'd never been so pleased to see anyone in her entire life...

'Emma... what the *hell* are you doing down there?' There was curt astonishment and relief in his voice in almost equal measures. He came down the rope ladder with the ease of an athlete. 'God, I've been searching everywhere for you! I was about to have the lake dragged!'

'You weren't...?' She whispered it ruefully as she pointed to her ankle and he inspected it with surprising gentleness.

'Well, it was a possibility,' he said abruptly. He met her eyes with a glitter of emotion she couldn't even begin to understand. 'Did you throw yourself down here hoping to end it all, Emma?' The trace of humour was bitter.

'No. I caught my foot in my dress and slipped,' she said unsteadily, 'and now I feel incredibly silly...'

'Come on, let's get out of here...' With apparent ease, he bent to lever her over his shoulder in the classic fireman's lift, and took her back up the ladder.

'Is the ball over? Have... have all the guests gone?' she managed, conscious of his strength as he carried her down to the bedroom.

'No. Our guests are still making merry. But I'm sure they'll excuse us from the rest of the evening.'

'You didn't really think I'd rushed off to end it all, did you?'

'Hardly. But we thought you could have had an accident. You were in a highly emotional state——'

'Don't patronise me, Dominick...'

'I am not patronising you,' he said quietly. He laid her on the bed in his room, and gazed down at her with a mixed expression. Something in his eyes made her heart contract with a stirring of response.

'Stay there and don't move,' he ordered softly. 'I'm going to tell the others I've found you, then I'm going to call Paul King straight away. He can take a look at your ankle.'

He was gone for only a few minutes. Emma, hardly conscious of her sore ankle, closed her eyes, and waited with mounting apprehension for the confrontation she knew must follow.

When he came back, he brought a tray with a bottle of Médoc and two glasses. He came to sit on the bed beside her, his eyes darkening as he took in her dishevelled appearance, the strained pallor of her face.

'I thought since you'd missed out on your last glass of wine downstairs I'd bring some up.' His tone was sardonic.

'Thanks...' She met his wry look with a sheepish smile, reddening slightly as she relived her very public flare of anger. 'That's...*considerate* of you. What...what made you look in the priest hole? Did you hear me shouting?'

'Not until I was on my way up. I just racked my brain to think where my neurotic little bride might have bolted to.'

'I'm *not* neurotic...' She trailed off at the grim expression in his eyes.

'I've never been so worried in my life, Emma. I thought you'd run out on me again. When I found your car still there, and I searched the house, I thought something might have happened to you...'

'It did. I fell down the priest hole,' she said with a slight smile. 'I...I suppose you want me to apologise for embarrassing you in front of all your guests?' she added, half bitter, half defiant. She wriggled backwards so that she was resting against the pillows as he passed her a glass of wine.

'No need. I imagine that I deserved it.'

The cool, flat retort took her totally by surprise. She stared at him uncomprehendingly.

'You think so?' Her expression was cautiously enquiring as she searched for some clue to his mood.

'It made me realise that pride was no way to glue my cracked marriage back together, Emma.'

'Pride...?'

'Pride. Ever since you flung your accusations at me, I've been behaving like an arrogant bastard. I've been waiting for you to come crawling back to me saying you trusted me...'

'Oh, Dominick...' She bit her lip miserably. 'I want to trust you! You don't know how much I want to...'

'Maybe you'd better read my father's will,' he suggested simply. He sat back, with a weary shrug of his shoulders. She suddenly registered how tired he looked. There were dark smudges under his eyes. His face looked drawn. The familiar lidded gaze held a bleakness which tugged at her heart.

'What are you saying?'

'Vanessa Buckingham is a brilliant lawyer. She's also a brilliant trouble-maker. But she had the facts wrong,' he said shortly, 'which I would have pointed out to you at the time if I hadn't been so furious with you for believing her in the first place. And if you hadn't complicated the whole damn thing by dragging your mother and my father into it.'

'Mrs Shields told me Sir Robert really loved my mother. But... that doesn't say much for his treatment of *your* mother, does it?'

Dominick flicked a long-suffering glance towards the ceiling.

'Let's leave all our parents, all our bloody awful relatives and ancestors, out of this, shall we?' His voice was grim. 'For my part, seeing my father's behaviour made me very hot on the notion of marital fidelity. I watched him live his life, and decided how *not* to live mine.'

She nodded slowly. 'That's the way I felt, too. About my mother's betrayal of Dad. It... it made me feel strongly about old-fashioned loyalty...'

'So what went wrong,' he probed hoarsely, 'with your loyalty to your new husband?'

She swallowed on a tight throat.

'Rushing into things?' she ventured miserably. 'Not knowing you well enough...'

'And not being prepared for Vanessa's muck-stirring.'

'That too...' She met his eyes again, with a despairing smile. 'So what were the facts she had wrong?'

'Richard didn't want the house, or estate,' he said shortly. 'He convinced my father of that. As eldest son, he'd automatically inherit the baronetcy. But his religious beliefs didn't tie in with material wealth. My father was worried that if Richard changed his mind, changed his lifestyle as he matured, he might regret the arrangement. Technically, the title, house and lands should have been his. So he wrote a special condition into his will. If Richard had married, settled back in England and wanted the manor, within two months of Sir Robert's death, he'd still be legally entitled to it. But only if he produced a child within a year of the marriage. That part was to ensure that Richard had truly abandoned his monastic leanings! Otherwise, Richard would get the title only. And the house and land was mine.'

She absorbed this in silence.

'So all the conditions applied to Richard? Only to Richard?' Her head was spinning.

'You can study the will with a magnifying glass if it will convince you,' Dominick said drily.

'So... you half expected to inherit the manor all along?'

'Yes. That's really why I was employing my new *archivist*, and taking such an interest,' Dominick agreed wryly. 'I expected Richard to stick to his guns. Follow his off-beat religious beliefs. I expected him to become the new twelfth baronet in his self-imposed Tibetan exile. I didn't expect him to die out there in Tibet without bloody well telling anyone!'

'Quite...' There was a taut silence.

Emma stared at the faded ochre-gold of the walls, at the old baroque-framed Turner-style seascapes hanging from the picture-rail.

'So... you didn't have to marry to inherit?'

'No, I didn't.'

'So... you married me because...'

'Because I wanted to marry you,' he supplied patiently. He shrugged off his dinner-jacket, as if he suddenly found the formal clothes unbearably constricting. The bow tie was dragged loose, the top button of his dress-shirt freed. The red wine had dried to an irregular stain, she saw guiltily. In the soft light of the bedroom, it resembled blood more than wine. She bit her lip hard, abruptly flooded with remorse.

'What...what made Vanessa think otherwise?' she probed carefully. This was awful. Like feeling her way, blindfold, through a maze of obstacles.

'Some wishful thinking,' he said quietly. 'She wanted there to be something between us that didn't exist for me. She was furious that I'd married you without even asking her to the wedding. And she had a sketchy half-knowledge of the legal conditions my father insisted on for my brother Richard. She put it all together, and decided that the speed of our marriage could only mean a kind of...marriage of convenience. Believe me, she knows where she stands. I wasn't in charge of selling tickets for tonight's ball, so I had no real power to stop her coming. But I made it clear that she should apologise to you, tonight.'

'But whenever I looked you were chatting and laughing together tonight. You both seemed to be so close, so friendly...!'

'I've been so bloody angry with you, I confess I paid her more attention than necessary tonight. Out of...petty pride and revenge?' His twist of bitter self-mockery made her heart seem to flip over in her chest.

'Really? How...how unkind to Vanessa,' she protested faintly.

'Nothing more than she deserves.' He spoke with a hint of ruthless anger. 'Besides, you weren't exactly kind to her yourself—with your "highly sexed" taunt.'

His eyes were midnight-dark, shadowed by the tired smudges beneath. Her pulses were racing suddenly. Her heart felt ready to explode...

'It was true, though, wasn't it?' she said huskily. 'You might not love me, but at least you...you *fancy* me?'

He took a swig of his wine, and his mouth thinned into a grim, lop-sided smile. But a hint of anger shone in his eyes.

'I find you extremely desirable. And who the hell said I don't love you?'

In the dim light he looked so ruggedly dark and handsome, the look in his eyes so blazingly masculine as they raked the length of her figure in the clinging silvery dress, that her stomach hollowed into total meltdown.

'You never told me you loved me...' she remonstrated huskily. 'Not even when I begged you to...'

'Cowardice,' he confessed quietly. 'In-built self-defence. Seeing what my parents did to each other. Not quite believing my luck, finding you...'

'What . . . what about Vanessa?' she breathed. 'How do you feel about her?'

'Emma . . .' his deep voice shook with sudden, taut emotion '. . . if I'd wanted Vanessa Buckingham, believe me I'd have married her years ago, before she embarked on the disastrous marriage she's just in the process of dissolving. She and I have been neighbours and friends for years. Whatever she feels about me, I've given her no encouragement. I don't love her. I don't even *fancy* her, as you so quaintly put it. Blondes aren't my type . . .'

'And I am?'

'Definitely,' he murmured hoarsely. 'Curvy brunettes with big grey eyes and endless legs are much more my taste . . .'

They stared at each other in tense silence. She was just shakily, warily reaching out to touch Dominick's hand, when there was a brief knock on the door and Paul King walked in, still in his shabby tweed jacket.

'I hope you're not going to make a habit of fainting and falling down priest holes, Lady Fleetwood,' he commented drily, after inspecting the ankle and pronouncing it a simple twist requiring only rest, 'or I can't guarantee the trouble-free pregnancy you'd otherwise enjoy.'

'God, the *baby*,' Dominick exclaimed unevenly, deep concern suddenly furrowing his forehead. 'I was so worried about Emma, I'd forgotten all about the baby! Is everything OK? Are you feeling all right, sweetheart . . . ?'

'Everything's fine.' The doctor straightened from his brief, practised feel of the soft curve of Emma's stomach and a check on her pulse, nodding reassuringly. 'Nothing a good night's sleep, plenty of rest and a little less adventurous exploring won't put right.'

Paul King gave Dominick a searching look as he prepared to leave. 'Make sure you take very good care of your new bride from now on, Sir Dominick,' he added, with a glint of humorous reproach.

'Don't worry,' Dominick retorted with soft vehemence, 'I intend to...'

When they were alone again, Dominick took her hands in his and held them tightly.

'Are you sure you're feeling all right?' he persisted huskily.

'Quite sure...' She hesitated, her throat annoyingly choked. 'I thought the baby was the most important thing to you,' she whispered uncertainly. 'Did you really forget...?'

'Temporarily...' His gaze was lidded, but brilliant with emotion. 'Emma, darling, I'm going to be the proudest father in the world when our child is born. The baby is incredibly important to me. But not more important than my wife...'

'Dominick...' The soft plea in her voice seemed to give him some kind of signal, because with a low curse under his breath he moved abruptly closer and took her in his arms.

'Emma, if I rushed you into marrying me, it was because I've never been so sure, never felt anything was so right,' he muttered, his voice terse against her hair. 'I wanted to make you mine. With no doubts or reservations. I sensed those reservations in you. That made speed even more important...'

'I had no reservations about loving you,' she whispered unsteadily. 'If I had any doubts, it was because of my mother, and your father. I felt confused about the past...'

'So you didn't marry me to avenge your mother? To make my life hell?' he murmured, inspecting her face with darkening eyes. 'Tonight's little scene at the ball wasn't just a taste of things to come?'

She shivered, her smile apologetic.

'No. I married you because... because you're the only man I'll ever want to marry. I feel very ashamed of myself tonight. I didn't even thank you properly for these...' She touched the diamond choker and earrings, her eyes shy on his intent, narrowed gaze.

'I bought you those when I was away for those three nights in London,' he told her drily, 'when we first got back from honeymoon. I couldn't wait to get back here and see you wearing them. But my homecoming didn't work out quite the way I'd planned, did it?'

Her stomach contracted with anguished guilt.

'Dominick, will you forgive me?' she whispered unsteadily.

'For throwing red wine at me? Or not trusting me?'

'Both.'

He shot her an ironic grin before kissing her, hard, on her trembling mouth.

'How the hell you could have believed that twisted rubbish from Vanessa I'll never know. And I doubt if I'll ever live down the red wine incident with Tobias and his cronies...'

'Cathy will tame your friend Tobias,' she whispered, with a soft laugh.

'True. I can see wedding-bells on the horizon for those two. And how can you ask me if I forgive you? Of course I forgive you!' he told her roughly. 'Emma, I love you. I'm crazy about you.'

'I love you too,' she whispered. His simple words had lifted her, like an invisible air-current. She was suddenly floating on a weightless cloud of happiness, so happy she felt she could fly, like Peter Pan and Wendy, out of the window and high into the night sky. 'I'm sorry I listened to Vanessa...'

'Forget her,' he breathed, searching for her mouth and hungrily raining short, provocative kisses on her softly parted lips. 'As my new bride, you're entitled to a second honeymoon. Where would you like to go?'

'But it's only about ten days since the first!' she laughed.

'Don't argue on technicalities. You need plenty of looking after. Doctor's orders...'

'How about taking the narrowboat along the river for a few days?' she suggested, smiling.

'How about a little Greek island in the sun? A fortnight of idle days and not so idle nights,' he countered with a wicked grin, stroking his hand down the curve of her neck to caress the swell of her breast.

'What will we do at night?' she teased. 'Play chess?'

He kissed her long and hard, flattening her decisively against the softness of the bed.

'I've a feeling that Paul's instructions about letting you get a good night's sleep will test my self-control tonight, my highly sexed little wife...'

'What self-control? You...' she laughed shakily, gazing up at him with starry eyes as bright as the diamonds '... are sex mad!'

'Only with you.'

For a long time, talking was out of the question. Then her ankle gave a sharp twinge. Her intake of breath made Dominick release her, full of remorse.

'The doctor's right,' he growled ruefully, his eyes on her bruised lips and tousled hair. 'You're in need of a good night's sleep, Lady Fleetwood...'

'That, my darling Sir Dominick,' she whispered, wriggling provocatively into the strength of his arms, 'is something *I'm* entitled to decide, don't you think...?'

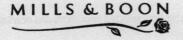

AND A MYSTERY GIFT

Return the coupon below and we'll send you 4 Mills & Boon romances absolutely FREE! We'll even pay the postage and packing for you.

We're making you this offer to introduce you to the benefits of Reader Service: FREE home delivery of brand-new Mills & Boon romances, at least a month before they are available in the shops, FREE gifts and a monthly Newsletter packed with information.

Accepting these FREE books places you under no obligation to buy, you may cancel at any time, even after receiving just your free shipment. Simply complete the coupon below and send it to:

HARLEQUIN MILLS & BOON, **FREEPOST**, PO BOX 70, CROYDON CR9 9EL.

Yes, please send me 4 Mills & Boon romances and a mystery gift as explained above. Please also reserve a subscription for me. If I decide to subscribe I shall receive 6 superb new titles every month for just £11.40* postage and packing free. I understand that I am under no obligation whatsoever. I may cancel or suspend my subscription at any time simply by writing to you, but the free books and gift will be mine to keep in any case. *I am over 18 years of age.*

NO STAMP NEEDED

1EP5R

Ms/Mrs/Miss/Mr _____

Address _____

_____

_____ Postcode _____

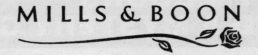

MILLS & BOON

Next Month's Romances

Each month you can choose from a wide variety of romance with Mills & Boon. Below are the new titles to look out for next month.

THE HEAT OF PASSION	Lynne Graham
SWEET SINNER	Diana Hamilton
UNWANTED WEDDING	Penny Jordan
THE BRIDE IN BLUE	Miranda Lee
FAITH, HOPE AND MARRIAGE	Emma Goldrick
PS I LOVE YOU	Valerie Parv
PARTNER FOR LOVE	Jessica Hart
VOYAGE TO ENCHANTMENT	Rosemary Hammond
HOLLOW VOWS	Alexandra Scott
DISHONOURABLE SEDUCTION	Angela Wells
TEMPTATION ON TRIAL	Jenny Cartwright
TO TAME A TEMPEST	Sue Peters
POTENT AS POISON	Sharon Kendrick
SHORES OF LOVE	Alex Ryder
DANGEROUS ATTRACTION	Melinda Cross
PASSIONATE RETRIBUTION	Kim Lawrence

Available from WH Smith, John Menzies, Volume One, Forbuoys, Martins, Woolworths, Tesco, Asda, Safeway and other paperback stockists.